"I'm afraid I must ask you to participate in a small charade."

Lady Roth sank down on the chaise longue. "If we cannot discover a way to prevent Emily from seeking out Mr. Carouthers, we must prevent him from seeking out Emily."

Becca was taken aback. "But I don't see how—"

"That," said Lady Roth, "is because you are not as crafty as I am, my dear. We shall simply offer him a more attractive catch."

"You mean find another heiress for him? Would it not be cruel, to betray another young innocent?"

"I would never do that, my dear, but you, I believe, will become an heiress in disguise. Immensely wealthy, helping us hide the fact that our fortune has diminished considerably. Our family connection will serve as a believable explanation for your generosity."

"Yes, Aunt," Becca said, but her thoughts were of Lucas. If she helped his sister, would it cost her the man she loved?

Regency England: 1811-1820

*"It was the best of times,
it was the worst of times...."*

As George III languished in madness, the pampered and profligate Prince of Wales led the land in revelry and the elegant Beau Brummell set the style. Across the Channel, Napoleon continued to plot against the English until his final exile to St. Helena. Across the Atlantic, America renewed hostilities with an old adversary, declaring war on Britain in 1812. At home, Society glittered, love matches abounded and poets such as Lord Byron flourished. It was a time of heroes and villains, a time of unrelenting charm and gaiety, when entire fortunes were won or lost on a turn of the dice and reputation was all. A dazzling period that left its mark on two continents and whose very name became a byword for elegance and romance.

Books by Judith Stafford

HARLEQUIN REGENCY ROMANCE
32—THE LEMON CAKE
51—A HERO'S WELCOME
62—CUPID AND THE VICAR

Don't miss any of our special offers. Write to us at the following address for information on our newest releases.

Harlequin Reader Service
U.S.: 3010 Walden Ave., P.O. Box 1325, Buffalo, NY 14269
Canadian: P.O. Box 609, Fort Erie, Ont. L2A 5X3

BECCA'S INDEPENDENCE
Judith Stafford

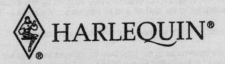

TORONTO • NEW YORK • LONDON
AMSTERDAM • PARIS • SYDNEY • HAMBURG
STOCKHOLM • ATHENS • TOKYO • MILAN • MADRID
PRAGUE • WARSAW • BUDAPEST • AUCKLAND

ISBN 0-373-31221-0

BECCA'S INDEPENDENCE

First North American Publication 1993.

This edition published by arrangement with Harlequin Books S.A.

Look us up on-line at: http://www.romance.net

Printed in U.S.A.

CHAPTER ONE

"WHOA, LUCAS! Are we in a race, of which you neglected to inform me?" Sir Anthony Burgess demanded as he grasped the side of the curricle.

Lord Roth grinned at his friend even as he slapped the reins against the backs of his matched bays. "Don't be absurd, Tony. I didn't take that corner too fast. You must've fallen asleep."

"I did not! Seriously, Lucas, why the rush?"

"I have a rendezvous with a widow." The dramatic utterance caused Sir Anthony to stare at his companion in astonishment. Lord Roth was the best of good friends, but he was not known for a hey-go-mad air, nor did he normally dangle after ripe widows.

"Did you imbibe too much ale at the inn?" Tony demanded.

Lucas Allenby, Lord Roth, eased back on the reins to avoid a farmer's cart before returning his attention to his companion. "Of course not. My sister is to be presented this Season and I must hire a companion for her."

"Your mother is still unable to get about?"

"She will never be able to do so," Roth returned, his tone grim. "She insisted on accompanying Emily to Town, much against my wishes, but I cannot allow her to become overset by the demands of a Season. Therefore, I am supposed to discover a suitable chaperon. The interviews were to commence this morning, but because of the problem at High Oaks, I asked Murdoch to have the ladies wait."

Sir Anthony tugged his many-caped coat closer to shut out the cold air. "I don't envy you," he assured his friend. Whether the shiver that accompanied his words was from the February cold or the prospect of a long row of widows, Lord Roth did not know.

"It should not be too onerous. The world is full of middle-aged widows in need of employment. I shall simply choose a sober, sensible woman to supervise Emily and continue on as before."

LADY REBECCA Jane Alexandra Dunlevy gripped her skirts tightly, keeping the hem away from the dirty floor of the hackney cab. Not that the dirt would much affect the dingy grey she wore. How she hated the gowns her aunt insisted were proper.

With a shudder, she stared out the small window of the cab. She had only been in London a few hours, and already she knew her aunt's views were not popular in the city. But while she'd finally escaped her aunt's control of her wardrobe, she'd embroiled herself in a difficult situation. Her father would have chastised her for her strong-headedness.

Stop it! she admonished herself as a sob rose in her throat. Self-pity was an indulgence she could not afford. And her father had been dead for almost two years.

The halting of the carriage shook her from her thoughts. She cautiously peered out the small window, relieved to see an elegant town house beside the hackney.

Gingerly turning the greasy knob on the door, she scrambled down before the driver, should he even have considered it, could assist her. He was even greasier than the knob.

Pulling the proper coinage from her reticule, Becca paid the man, all the while wondering what would become of her if she did not gain the position of companion to the lady who resided here in such splendour. Her money would not go far if she had to pay for many carriage rides.

"Thank 'ee. Want me to wait for yer?"

"Oh, no, thank you. I—I am expected."

The half-truth slipped easily from her lips. *I am becoming an accomplished liar.* That was another fault her father would have condemned.

Mr. Fishbait, the old gentleman at the hire firm where her father had always sought out her governesses, had assured her the Earl of Roth was interviewing for a chaperon today, but he had not held out much hope that Becca would be chosen for the position.

As Rebecca Dunn, a young countrywoman come to London to seek employment, she had little to recommend her other than her beauty. And the elderly man had felt that in itself was a fault that might hinder her employment. Even when she invented a dead husband so she might qualify as a widow, a requirement for this position, he had discouraged her hopes.

However, Becca had a secret Mr. Fishbait did not know. She was a distant relation of the potential employer: Lady Roth's husband had been a nephew to her mother's uncle by marriage.

She'd intended to hold the Roths in reserve, as a last resort if she were unable to find a position. It was a lowering thought to have to throw oneself on a distant family connection.

Mr. Fishbait had had no other position available. When she heard the name of the family seeking a chaperon, she'd felt Fate nudging her to this place. She only hoped the Roths wouldn't try to verify her relationship to them, for they might discover her true identity. As distant as the connection was, she now hoped that it might improve her chances for the position.

Becca lifted her chin, a movement familiar to those who knew her, and walked up the steps. She *must* get this position. She didn't want to have to beg for a place to sleep that night.

In response to her knock, a dignified butler invited her to enter and state her business. When she offered Mr. Fishbait's card, he stared at her in surprise before gesturing towards an empty chair. It was then that Becca noticed the two other women, their grim expressions trained on her face.

"Please be seated. Lord Roth has been delayed."

Becca sat down next to her competition. Her smile was ignored and she sank her bottom teeth into her lip as her fervent prayers quietly winged their way Heavenwards.

"I AM STILL NOT SURE we should continue, Emily," Lady Roth said.

"We will not if you are too tired, Mama, but—but we cannot leave the choice to Lucas. He would have hired that Mrs. Majors if he'd interviewed her. Or the other one, whatever her name was."

The ladies, one delicate and middle-aged, the other a petite blond beauty of only seventeen, exchanged a look of horror.

"Can you imagine living with either of them?" Lady Roth whispered. "I don't believe they have smiled in years."

Emily shrugged her shoulders. "Our house is not such a merry place as to notice, Mama."

Lady Roth nibbled on her bottom lip. "I am sorry, my child. I suppose life has been rather grim for you during the past two years."

"Oh, Mama," the young lady cried, dashing across the room to sink to her knees and embrace her mother. Lady Roth was lying on a *chaise longue,* her limbs hidden from view by a coverlet. "I did not mean to complain. It is you who has suffered the most. I have felt so cut off from you. After Papa...after Papa died—"

Before she could continue, a cool voice asked, "Am I intruding? The butler said I was to enter."

Both ladies looked up in surprise to see a tall young woman, a stunning beauty, gazing at them.

Emily clutched her mother's hand as she rose to her feet. Lady Roth stared at the young woman even as she gestured to a nearby chair. "Of course you are not intruding. Please, be seated. You—you *are* here about the position?"

"Why, yes." The woman leaned forward as she sat down, her black curls framing her delicate features. "Has it been filled?"

Emily took a step closer. "*You* want to be a chaperon?"

A wide smile spread across her face, making her more entrancing, if possible. "I don't precisely *want* to become a chaperon, but I must find employment."

"But, my dear, you are so young," Lady Roth said.

A more cautious look entered the green eyes. "How old must I be?"

"Why—why, I don't believe we specified an age. Lucas just assumed if he advertised for a widow, she would be...older." Lady Roth's fingers plucked at the coverlet before asking, "You are a widow, aren't you?"

Looking suitably saddened, the newcomer said, "Yes, my lady. I lost my husband several years ago."

"Of course she is, Mama, or she would not be wearing that dreadful grey," Emily added, trying to be helpful.

"Emily!" Lady Roth protested. "You should not be so impolite."

"It is frightful, isn't?" the young lady agreed with a grin.

Lady Emily Allenby needed no more information. She would no longer dread the Season if she had the company of this lady. "Mama, we must hire her. She is perfect."

The two young ladies exchanged hopeful smiles, but the unknown applicant waited for the older woman's verdict.

"I—I admit she is a delightful young woman, Emily, but she is so young. I beg your pardon, my dear, but I do not *even* know your name."

"It is Rebecca Dunn, my lady. Mrs. Jeremy Dunn. I should also mention that I am a—a distant connection," she added with modest reluctance. "Of course, I do not expect such to affect your decision."

Lady Roth raised her eyebrows in surprise. "A connection? You are related to us?"

"My grandmother's sister married a Mr. Henry Allenby a number of years ago. I never met her," she hurriedly added, "but I have several of her letters to Grandmother."

"Uncle Henry? You were kin to Aunt Louisa!" Lady Roth smiled warmly. "She was not such a beauty as you, my dear, but I do see a faint resemblance. How wonderful! A member of our family!"

"The connection is distant, my lady."

"Nonsense, child. I am so sorry you have been reduced to such straits. How did your husband...that is, er—"

"He died of a fever, my lady."

"Oh, you poor child. To be widowed so young."

"See, Mama, she is exactly as Lucas ordered. *And* she is part of our family."

"We are delighted to have found you, child, and hope you will remain with us." But before the two young ladies could express the excitement evident on their faces, she added, "I do not know, however, if Lucas will allow you to fulfil the role of chaperon."

Joy left Mrs. Dunn's face. "I cannot remain without earning my keep, my lady. I would do my best to serve you."

"I'm sure you would, child, but—" Hesitancy marked the older woman's face as her gaze swung from her daughter to the other young lady. "Very well. We shall continue with the interview as if you were not a connection of ours. Have you had experience of the Season?"

"No, ma'am."

"Oh, dear. Have you managed a household? I mean, a large one? I know those duties are not usual for a chaperon, but Lucas—" She broke off abruptly. Then, "I hoped whoever we hired might be able to guide Emily in the art of keeping house."

"Yes, I have done so for several years."

"Your husband had a large estate?" A worried frown settled on Lady Roth's brow.

"No, my lady. My husband was not well-to-do, but after his death, I—I was companion to an elderly lady near Nottingham. When she died, I decided to come to London." She finished with a triumphant air, as if she had accomplished a difficult task.

"Do you have references?"

"Mama!" Emily protested. "Surely that is not—"

"Yes, my lady. I do not have references from my previous employer because she died, but a dear friend, the daughter of an earl, has written a letter of reference for me."

"Oh, good. That might help convince Lucas, since you are so young. If I might see it?"

The young lady retrieved a much-folded sheet from her reticule and handed it to Lady Roth. While the elder lady perused the reference, she and Emily exchanged smiles.

"Well, I'm sure there is nothing that Lucas can object to other than your being rather young. How old are you?"

Mrs. Dunn looked at each of the ladies before saying hesitantly, "Twenty-four?"

"It is not a riddle, silly," Emily said with a chuckle, liking her new companion more and more.

"No, of course not. I was only hoping that I am old enough. I will work very hard," she added, smiling at Lady Roth.

"Of course, child, as if that would be necessary. And I'm sure Lucas will understand about your age...and your lack of experience...especially since you are a family connection. You are sure you want this position? It is not necessary, since—''

"I would be most pleased, my lady," she said, her delightful smile underlining her pleasure.

Lady Roth could only smile in return. Surely Lucas would understand. "Very well, my dear Mrs. Dunn. You shall be Emily's companion for the Season."

"Oh, Mama, thank you!" Emily squealed in excitement, kissing her mother soundly. "Shall I show Mrs. Dunn to her room?"

"Yes, please, darling. I—I shall visit with you again after you have settled in, Mrs. Dunn."

The two young women left the room, already chattering like old friends. Lady Roth subsided against her pillows, afraid she'd made a decision of which Lucas would not approve.

"WHAT A LOVELY ROOM," Becca involuntarily exclaimed as Emily escorted her into a bedchamber farther along the corridor.

"It is just across the hall from mine. I think Lucas hoped a chaperon's near presence would prevent me from misbehaving."

Rebecca ignored the disturbing hint of her charge's intentions and asked another question. "Who is Lucas?"

Emily subsided on the *chaise longue* near the window. "My brother," she said with a groan.

Recognizing the tone, Rebecca leaned forward. "Is he so dreadful?"

"Not to mere mortals. But he is horrible to me!"

Since Emily did not have the air of one frequently beaten or starved, Becca's sympathy was limited. "Why?"

"I do not know. After Papa's death, Lucas turned into a veritable monster. He wouldn't let me visit with Mama or go anywhere. I have scarce even been shopping in two years."

"But surely he would not keep you from your mother? You were together this morning."

"Oh, he is only trying to take care of her." At the puzzled look on Rebecca's face, Emily explained, "She was crippled in the accident that killed Papa. She cannot walk."

"Oh, no! How distressing!"

"Yes. So you see, Lucas didn't want me to bother her. As if I would!" She grimaced and shrugged her shoulders, perhaps acknowledging that she might have, if given the chance. "Anyway, that is the reason for hiring you. Mama wanted someone to accompany me during the Season."

"But I know no one. I shall not be able to introduce you to Society." Rebecca frowned, wondering if her employment would be short-lived.

"That is of no consequence. My aunt lives here in London, and Mama has many friends who will provide introductions. You are only supposed to keep an eye on me and assist me in selecting a wardrobe. Mama thinks Aunt Cynthia is too muddle-headed to remember to keep track of me." Emily laughed in agreement with her mother. "Sometimes Aunt Cynthia has difficulty remembering her own children."

"I think I am capable of looking out for you, and of assisting with the purchase of your wardrobe," Rebecca assured her with a smile.

"Of course you are. Well, I shall leave you to rest," Emily said. As she reached the door, she paused. "Must I call you Mrs. Dunn?"

"You may call me Becca when we are alone, as my—my friends call me."

"Wonderful! I am so glad you have come, Becca, or perhaps I should say, Cousin Becca!" Emily added before slipping from the room.

In spite of her delight with the bedchamber and her enjoyment of Emily's company, Becca acknowledged that her position would be no sinecure, even though they had readily accepted her as a member of the family. Keeping Lady Emily from making *faux pas* would not be easy. Especially when she herself did not know the rules of Society.

Guilt filled her as she realized her inexperience might hurt the young lady. But she could not refuse the position. Having run away from her own home, she had nowhere else to go.

"MURDOCH, allow me a few minutes to compose myself and then show in the first of the candidates," Lord Roth said as he handed his butler his outer garments.

The butler nervously cleared his throat. "Er, my lord, Lady Roth interviewed the candidates."

A dark frown settled on his forehead. "Very well. I shall confer with her before making my decision. Five minutes," he added as he strode down the hall.

"My lord!" Murdoch called, halting his employer in his tracks. "My lady dismissed all the candidates but one."

Lord Roth turned slowly to stare at his butler. "And where is the remaining candidate?"

"I—I believe Lady Emily showed her to the chamber set aside for the chaperon." Murdoch saw the gathering storm on Lord Roth's face and wanted no responsibility for its birth.

Stunned by the information the butler related, Lord Roth pressed his lips tightly together and only nodded to the man. "Very well." Without another word, he ran up the stairs, taking two at a time, and turned down the corridor to his mother's chamber.

His rap on the door was answered by Eva, the large woman who attended his mother's every need. "I must speak with Lady Roth," he said pleasantly, not letting any irritation show in his voice or face.

The woman moved back, allowing him to enter. When she did not exit in turn, he added, "Privately, please, Eva."

Lady Roth, still on the *chaise longue,* followed her servant's departure with her eyes before she faced her son. "Hello, my dear. Did you take care of the difficulty at High Oaks?"

"Yes, I did," he said, leaning over to kiss her cheek. "And I understand from Murdoch you dealt with everything here."

"He told you that I hired a companion," Lady Roth murmured.

"Actually, no. He said you dismissed the other candidates." He settled himself on a nearby chair and looked at his mother expectantly.

"Oh, Lucas, they were terrible. Neither Emily nor I could bear the thought of their company."

One eyebrow arched in speculation, but he only said, "I am happy you found someone to please you." His curiosity intensified when his mother's cheeks flushed, and he added, "I had hoped to save you the trouble of choosing a companion, you know. I told Murdoch to ask the ladies to wait."

Lady Roth plucked at her coverlet, her gaze dropping from the piercing blue eyes which were fixed on her. "Well," she said, licking her suddenly dry lips, "Emily and I thought, since we would be the ones spending the most time with the companion, that we should choose someone we both liked."

"And how long did it take Emily to convince you?" he asked, his voice gentle in spite of its ironic tone.

A reluctant smile flitted across his mother's face and Lord Roth realized her smile had not been much in evidence during the past two years.

"It *was* Emily's idea, I confess, but I believe she has the right of it. *You* will not be in the woman's company more than once a week. Emily and I, on the other hand, will be spending our every waking moment with her."

"I agree, except that it is Emily who will be spending time with the woman. You will not. Just because I allowed you to come to London does not mean that I will let you exhaust yourself over that silly child." He stood and kissed his mother's cheek again before turning to the door.

"Lucas," Lady Roth called, "you will accept our choice?"

He smiled lovingly back at his mother. "I am no monster, Mama. If you and Emily are satisfied with the lady, and she is properly trained for the position, then of course I shall accept your choice."

After leaving his mother's chamber, Lord Roth crossed the hall and knocked on another door. "Emily? I would have a word with you."

Lady Emily opened her door cautiously. "Yes?"

"I would remind you that our mother is an invalid and not up to the rigours of daily life. You should have told me you wished to confer on my choice of companion." He did not bother to hide his irritation with his sister as he had with his mother.

"You would not have listened!" Emily exclaimed. "You never do."

"And you must stop behaving like a child. I expect you to have a greater consideration for our mother."

"I love Mama!" she replied, tears spurting from her eyes. "I did not hurt her."

"Perhaps not. But in future you will deal with me, not Mama. Is that understood?" His stern visage left no room for argument.

"Yes," she said, her lips turned down at the corners. As her brother turned to leave, she quickly asked, "But Mrs. Dunn may remain as my chaperon?"

He turned around to study his sister's eager face. The woman must be a miracle worker to bring such enthusiasm to both the ladies in his household. "Yes, if she is your choice and is qualified for the position." A niggling worry made him add the second stipulation. Both his mother and sister seemed to expect him to turn the woman out at once. Surely they did not think him quite so unreasonable.

"She is a widow, isn't she?" he asked.

"Oh, yes. Her husband died of a fever several years ago."

"And how has she occupied her time since his death?"

"She was companion to an elderly lady in Nottingham. And she ran her large household also," Emily added for good measure, hoping to impress her brother.

"Good. Then she will be able to instruct you in that particular art, as well as provide chaperonage."

"Of course, Lucas. I'm sure she will be an excellent teacher."

Nodding, he turned to go, but his sister's enthusiasm made him wonder about the new companion. He should interview the woman at once, but he had promised Tony he would dine with him before they went to the theatre. He'd talk with the new chaperon tomorrow.

BECCA HAD JUST FINISHED stowing away her garments in the capacious cupboards that lined one wall of her chamber when someone knocked on her door.

"Have you rested?" Emily asked after Becca had invited her to enter.

"No, I unpacked."

"You should not have. A servant could have done it for you."

"It is all right. I have little." And all of it that miserable grey that her aunt and uncle had insisted was proper. She shuddered, just thinking about the change in her life since her father's death. Her new guardians were followers of the Noncomformists, a new name for the Puritans who had once overthrown the Crown. Now they occupied themselves with saving the world from its sins. An admirable goal, Becca willingly acknowledged. But she did not understand why one must wear the hated grey to rescue others.

Noticing her shudder, Emily asked, "You are cold? I shall have a fire built at once."

"No, no, I was just…remembering."

"A fire should have been lit for you anyway. Lucas may sometimes be difficult, but he is not a nip cheese."

"Do you think he will approve of my taking the position?" Becca asked.

"He has already said you may stay if you are my choice," Emily assured her, ignoring the qualification her brother had added.

"How generous of him."

"Yes. Now, shall we go down to dinner? We are keeping country hours until the Season begins."

Becca looked down at her plain grey dress. "Will your brother mind my attire? I'm afraid it is all I have."

"Murdoch said he will be out, so it will just be the two of us."

"Your mother will not join us?"

"Lucas does not like her to strain herself by leaving her chamber. She always dines there."

Though such a plan sounded terribly dull to Becca, she kept her thoughts to herself. She was relieved to discover she would not have to face Lord Roth on this, her first night, at least.

The two young ladies descended the stairs and entered the parlour to await Murdoch's summons. They chatted about everyday events, learning of each other's likes and dislikes, and discovering, much to their pleasure, many similarities. By the time Murdoch led them across the foyer to the dining-room, they were fast becoming friends.

The sound of steps on the stairs drew Becca's eye as she followed in Murdoch's wake. She paused automatically as she faced a most handsome gentleman, his tall form manly yet graceful, his blond curls casually framing a broad forehead above brilliant blue eyes.

The only flaw in his appearance, in Becca's eyes, was the stark black coat and trousers he wore with a pristine white shirt and neckcloth. Surely he could not be a Noncomformist like her guardians, forbidding bright, cheery colours. When her father had dressed for the evening he had chosen brilliant silks and satins.

The man, too, stopped and stared at her, seemingly as surprised as she. Though she did not look away, Becca sensed Emily's return to her side, and she waited for an introduction.

Emily remained silent, and the handsome gentleman on the stairs took command of the situation. "Emily, will you not introduce your guest? I do not believe I have had the good fortune to make her acquaintance."

Some foreboding warned Becca of the gentleman's identity, but she looked to her new friend for confirmation.

"This is my brother, Lord Roth. Lucas, may I present Mrs. Dunn, my ch-chaperon."

Astonishment, quickly followed by anger, replaced the admiration on his face.

CHAPTER TWO

THE GENTLEMAN'S FACE was wiped clean of all emotion. "Might we converse in the parlour?" Lord Roth asked, steel edging his innocuous question.

The two young ladies, after exchanging an apprehensive look, retraced their footsteps.

"Dinner will be delayed, Murdoch," Lord Roth said before he closed the door behind him.

Becca was afraid her delightful position was about to end and she would be turned out on the street, homeless. Telling herself she should have known finding a place would not be so easy, she turned to face the gentleman.

"You are the widow they hired as a chaperon?" Lord Roth asked, ignoring his sister.

"Yes, my lord."

He stared at her before repeating, "You are a widow?"

"Yes, my lord." She dropped her gaze to her hands, clasped tightly in front of her to keep them from shaking.

"Lucas—" Emily said, trying to intervene.

"One moment, please, Emily. I suppose you have been through a Season?"

Becca's semblance of serenity was slipping away. "No, my lord."

Astounded, Lord Roth's gaze swung from the beautiful young woman to his sister's hopeful face and back again. "You have no experience, you are much too young and...too beautiful, and yet they hired you?" His brows rose in mock surprise as he looked again at his sister before turning back to Mrs. Dunn.

Becca's cheeks paled, but she returned his look.

"Lucas, Becca is wonderful and we are very happy with her."

He ignored his sister's words, his gaze remaining on Becca. She did not understand the strange gleam in his eyes, a gleam that he quickly suppressed. "My apologies, Mrs. Dunn. I'm afraid I cannot allow you to remain as my sister's chaperon. You will be suitably recompensed in the morning."

Becca took her dismissal silently, but Emily did not. "No! Lucas, you cannot—"

"I'm afraid it will not do, Emily. Mrs. Dunn does not have the requirements for a chaperon, though, of course, she is charming." He gave a slight bow in her direction. "I shall await your convenience in the morning, Mrs. Dunn." Without another word, he turned and strode from the parlour.

A single tear escaped from Becca's eye as she sank her teeth into her bottom lip. She had hoped—ah, well, it mattered little now. Tomorrow, she must seek a new hiding place.

"No! He must not... Come, Becca!"

Startled, Becca followed Emily. "Where are you going, Emily?"

"To Mama. She will stop Lucas!"

Emily was halfway up the stairs, having passed a startled Murdoch in the foyer, before Becca caught up with her. "Emily, you must not upset your mother."

"I am not going to see my Season ruined just because my precious brother does not understand!" She surged ahead, with Becca reluctantly following in her wake.

In response to Emily's knock, Eva opened the door slightly, her large body blocking their view. "You cannot come in. Her ladyship has retired for the evening."

"Mama!" Emily called, ignoring the servant.

"Eva, is it Emily? Open the door, please."

Eva's face showed her reluctance to obey the faint voice they had all heard, but she did so. Stepping aside, she allowed the two young ladies to enter.

Propped up by pillows in her large bed, Lady Roth appeared smaller and more fragile than ever. Becca felt guilty about being the cause of the disturbance.

"Mama! Lucas saw Becca and dismissed her!" Emily exclaimed, clasping the frail hand lying on the coverlet in her own strong fingers.

"Oh, dear. I was hoping he would not see her until I had spoken to him again." Lady Roth's gaze sought Becca's. "He did not upset you, did he, child?"

"Of course not, my lady. I am distressed that I must seek another position, but I understand—"

"Well, I do not." Emily knelt beside the bed. "Mama, please make Lucas understand. Becca is—is like a friend. I have been so lonely the last two years. Since Becca has come, I have been happy. And she is part of our family!"

"Child, she has only been here a few hours, but you are right, of course. I did not have the opportunity to inform Lucas of our connection." Lady Roth explained to Becca and her daughter. "And what is it she is calling you?" she asked Becca.

"I asked her to call me Becca, my lady. It is short for Rebecca."

"It is charming, my dear." She patted her daughter's hand before asking, "Mrs. Dunn, are you willing to stay?"

"Of course, my lady, if Lord Roth agrees. I would be delighted." And greatly relieved.

"Please, Mama?"

"Of course, child. I am sure Lucas will agree once I have explained everything to him. Do not be concerned, Mrs. Dunn."

"Thank you, my lady."

"Thank you, Mama, you are marvellous. We shall go back down to dinner and leave you in peace."

As they turned to go, something in her employer's expression caused Becca to ask, "You have eaten, have you not, my lady?"

"I did not have an appetite."

"Why do you not join us at table? If it is only the three of us, I'm sure you may dine *en déshabillé*."

"Emily may not have told you, Becca, but I cannot walk."

Becca smiled faintly. "Yes, she told me, my lady, but that is no reason for you to remain a prisoner in your chamber. I would have no appetite either, if I stared at the same four walls every day."

"But how…" Lady Roth, words trailed off, but both young ladies noticed the colour rising in her cheeks.

"What a capital idea, Becca. We'll get one of the footmen to carry you to table, Mama! It will be wonderful!"

Lady Roth made no protest, a look of excitement on her face, and in no time the young ladies had put their plan into action. Once seated at the table, Lady Roth found her appetite returned and she ate heartily, accompanied by much laughter and chatter.

After dinner, she asked her daughter and Becca to accompany her to her bedchamber. "My dears, I have been thinking. We should make plans now for the redecoration of the house and the purchase of Emily's wardrobe, so that I might convince Lucas our decision is a good one."

"Are you sure you are not too tired, my lady?" Becca asked, watching her for signs of exhaustion.

"No, Becca, I feel better than I have in days, or even months."

For almost an hour, lists were drawn up and plans

laid. When Becca assumed Lady Roth would accompany them to purchase gowns for Emily, Lady Roth found herself agreeing, though with a some reservation.

"Will not people think it strange to see me carried by a footman?"

"They may be surprised the first time, but they will soon become accustomed to it. Do you not wish to go out? Surely you have taken carriage rides? I understand it is quite the fashionable thing to do in London."

"Yes, when the Season begins. It is too chilly now. But you are right. There is no reason I cannot ride in a carriage. No one would even know I could not walk if I were in a carriage," she said with wonderment in her eyes.

After a few more minutes, Becca insisted they lay aside their plans and allow Lady Roth to retire. "We do not want to exhaust you before we have even begun."

Lady Roth clasped Becca's hand, a faint smile on her lips. "I believe, my dear, that you are going to be very good for us. Tonight I shall sleep like a baby."

"I hope so, my lady."

"Good night, Mama. It has been a wonderful evening."

"Yes, darling, it has."

In the hallway, Emily turned and hugged a surprised Becca. "If I did not love you for myself, I would love you for Mama. She has not appeared so happy since the accident. She greatly enjoyed dining with us.''

''I am glad she agreed to. She is a delightful lady.'' Becca smiled at her new friend. ''But we must remember she is fragile and tires easily.''

''You almost sound like Lucas,'' Emily protested with a laugh. ''But I shall not forget. Good night, Becca. I shall see you in the morning.''

BECCA WAS NOT SURE what constituted morning in her new household. In the country, one did not sleep until noon as she had heard Londoners were wont to do. By nine o'clock, she could stay in her room no longer. She went quietly down the stairs to discover Murdoch in the foyer, just emerging from the butler's pantry.

''Good morning, Mrs. Dunn.''

''Good morning, Murdoch. I do not wish to be a bother, but might I find something for breakfast in the kitchen?''

Shocked, the butler stammered, ''Th-there's no need to go to the kitchen, Mrs. Dunn. Breakfast is laid in the breakfast parlour whenever you desire it.''

''Oh, thank you. I was afraid the family might not arise until noon.'' With a sunny smile, Becca followed his directions to a small room draped in blue chintz with French doors opening out to the narrow garden behind the town house.

''How charming!''

"Yes, madam. I'll fetch hot water for tea."

Becca found various dishes on the sideboard and filled her plate. As she finished, Murdoch returned to pour her tea and she settled in to enjoy a delightful breakfast.

Halfway through, Becca's repast was interrupted by the arrival of Lord Roth. Sauntering into the room, he was almost to the sideboard before he realized there was another person present. "I beg your pardon. I did not see you at first. It is Mrs. Dunn, is it not?"

She nodded, a cautious smile on her face.

In truth, he had forgotten neither her name nor her face. He had been stunned by her beauty the previous evening, as much as he had been by her lack of qualifications.

"I hope Murdoch has provided for your needs?"

"Yes, my lord."

"Good. Now, have you made arrangements for another position?"

"No, my lord. There has been no time."

"No, of course not. Well, if we can be of assistance in any way, please let me know."

Becca nodded, and silence fell as Lord Roth sat down and began his breakfast.

Though nothing else was said, Lord Roth was all too aware of his breakfast companion. Her elegant hands drew his gaze as she poured more tea. Her green eyes were large and dewy, surrounded by lush black lashes. When she caught his eyes upon her, warm colour flooded her porcelain cheeks.

He applied himself to his eggs. It was a good thing she was leaving, he told himself. Such an attractive chaperon would draw attention away from his sister.

"You are very young to be a widow." Somehow he could not picture her in widow's weeds, though her grey gown was almost as dismal.

"Death can occur at any age, my lord."

The young lady kept her eyes lowered and Lord Roth stared at her as she continued to eat. "Have you no family with which to take refuge?"

That question brought her gaze to her inquisitor, and he lost himself in the green depths of her eyes. What an exquisite beauty she was!

She took overly long to respond to his question, he thought, but she finally answered, "No, my lord."

Her gaze returned to her breakfast as one of his eyebrows rose questioningly. "Surely even a distant connection would provide assistance, relieving you of the necessity to seek a position." The thought of turning such an exquisite beauty out of his house troubled him, but she was completely inappropriate as Emily's chaperon.

"I can provide for myself, my lord," she assured him. Before he could reply, she touched the napkin to her full lips and rose from the table. "If you will excuse…"

A loud commotion from belowstairs interrupted her speech and she remained standing, her eyes wide with surprise.

"What the—" Lord Roth swallowed the oath he'd

been about to mutter and stood also. Immediately, Murdoch appeared in the doorway.

"Excuse me, my lord, there's been a disaster in the kitchen and Monsieur Henri has resigned." His rushed speech and bright eyes indicated his concern.

"Dam—dash it all!" Lord Roth exclaimed. "What is the matter with that blasted cook? He has resigned three times this week!"

"French chefs are known to be temperamental," Becca said softly.

"Oh? And do you know how to deal with such a one?" he asked as his eyes traced her slim but well-rounded figure.

She met his gaze with a slight smile. "I have done so in the past." Her father had insisted on having a French chef, but it had taken a great deal to satisfy him, since they lived so far from London and seldom entertained. It had been her responsibility from the age of ten to placate the man.

"Very well, I would appreciate your assistance in the matter, Mrs. Dunn. I will add a reward to your payment when you leave if you can convince the man to stay."

With only a nod, Becca circled the table and paused beside the butler. "If you please, Murdoch, will you show me to the kitchen?"

In the blink of an eye, Lord Roth found himself alone, and he resettled himself at the table. The lady had accepted his challenge quite calmly. He could not picture Emily doing so. Of course, his sister was some years younger and had had little experience in such matters. Their housekeeper at High Oaks had held that position for years and had continued on as before when her mistress had been injured.

But while Mrs. Dunn might teach Emily about housekeeping, she still would not be suitable as a companion. Even if she were older, as long as her appearance did not change, she would outshine his little sister.

Not that Emily was unattractive. But compared to Mrs. Dunn's extraordinary beauty, his sister's looks seemed merely pale prettiness.

The reappearance of the lady, along with his butler, surprised him. "What? You have given up already?" he demanded, a superior smile on his face as he stood.

Becca only curtsied, but one eyebrow rose at his assumption.

"Oh, no, my lord," Murdoch hastened to explain. "Why, Mrs. Dunn had that Frenchie wrapped around her finger in no time. She smoothed his feathers completely."

Lord Roth turned and gave a formal bow to the young lady. "My compliments, Mrs. Dunn, and my thanks. I shall see to it that you are suitably recompensed."

"Thank you, my lord. If you will excuse me?"

At his nod, she slipped from the room. Immediately, he turned to his butler. "What did she say to the man?"

"I don't rightly know, my lord. She spoke to him

like a Frenchie. But whatever she said pleased him mightily."

"Well, it is too bad she is leaving."

Murdoch looked at his employer in surprise. "Leaving? After her being so good for Lady Roth, I thought—"

"What do you mean?"

"Why, nothing, my lord, except that Lady Roth had a much better appetite last evening when she dined downstairs."

"What? My mother dined downstairs?" He stood, shoving back his chair. "How?"

"Jem, one of the footmen, carried her."

Without another word, Lord Roth rushed from the breakfast room to his mother's bedchamber. Admitted into her presence by Eva, he hurried over to the bed.

"Mother? Are you all right?"

Having just finished a leisurely breakfast with more appetite than she'd had of late, Lady Roth was feeling at her best. "All right? Of course I am, dear. Why would I not be?"

"Murdoch told me you dined downstairs last evening. I was afraid it would be too much for you. Did Emily insist that you do so? I shall speak to her at once. I have warned her—"

"Lucas! Remain calm. Can you not see that I am all right?" She gave him her best smile and dared him with her eyes to disagree.

He smiled in return and bent to kiss her cheek. "Very well, I agree that you are in fine fettle, but how did such a thing occur? Eva has strict orders to coddle you, you know.''

"Eva has orders to imprison me," Lady Roth said lightly, avoiding her son's eyes. When he did not respond to her harsh words, she looked up at him apologetically.

"I never intended—"

"I know you did not, darling. And in the first months after the accident and your father's death, I needed the precious care you gave me. But lately, I have been feeling—oh, I don't know. Restless, perhaps."

"But you said nothing," he protested, concern creasing his brow.

"I did not realize the difficulty myself. It was only last night, when Becca asked me to dine with them, that I realized how...how lonely I was, how bored with my own company."

Lord Roth drew in a deep breath. "Very well, Mama. We shall try to keep you better entertained. Perhaps once a week you may come down to dinner."

"I have a better idea, darling." Lady Roth smiled at her beloved son, an impish look in her eye that surprised him.

With foreboding he asked, "What is it?"

"Allow us to keep Mrs. Dunn as Emily's companion."

"No! That is impossible!" he exclaimed. He began pacing the length of his mother's bedchamber. "You have not thought, Mama. Such a decision would ruin Emily's Season.''

"How so?"

"She is too young! She has no experience of a London Season and…and she is too beautiful!'' His cheeks reddened as he added his last complaint, and his mother looked at him speculatively.

"She is certainly very attractive, but your sister has her own charms, you know. I think they will make a delightful pair.''

"No one will even *see* Emily if Mrs. Dunn is in the same room.''

"Darling, you may not hold your sister's charms in high esteem, but I can assure you others will. In addition to her beauty, she also has a handsome portion. Emily will fare well in the Marriage Mart, and she is so much happier in Becca's company. Last evening was delightful.''

Before her son could voice the refusal written on his face, she added, "Also, I forgot to tell you last evening that Becca is a family connection. She is kin to Aunt Louisa. We could not turn her out, and she insists she will not remain unless she can be of some service to us.''

Lord Roth groaned as he tried to marshal his thoughts. His mother was right: they could not cast a member of their family out into the street. Becca— Rebecca, he assumed—Dunn must remain in his home, under his protection.

"Please, darling, to make me happy?''

He had spent a great deal of effort the past two years in an attempt to please his mother. With a sigh, he nodded. Under the circumstances, he had no choice.

"Oh, thank you, Lucas. Ring the bell for Eva. She must summon the girls. They will both be so pleased. I know you will agree with us as soon as you are acquainted with Becca. She is such a delight!"

CHAPTER THREE

FOR THE NEXT several weeks, as February turned to March and London came alive with those returning for the Season, Lord Roth avoided both his home and the ladies residing there. After leaving strict instructions with Murdoch and Eva for his mother's care, he spent time at each of his three estates.

The ladies residing at Roth House took advantage of his absence to grow more closely acquainted and to put into operation their plans for refurbishing the town house and themselves. Becca daily gave thanks for having found a position where she had gained the one thing she most longed for: a family.

Since her father's death, she had missed the companionship and love she had shared with him. Her aunt and uncle had been kind, as long as she conformed to their beliefs and did not disturb their routines. But that was not companionship.

Lady Roth and Emily, however, had become her companions as well as her friends, and she enjoyed her time in their company. Rather than considering her an employee or a poor relation, they treated her as a true member of the family.

Upon their first visit to a dressmaker, Madame

Printemps, the latest in a long line of French couturières the ton flocked to, Lady Roth demonstrated her feelings for Becca.

"Madame Printemps, we must have a complete wardrobe for my two young ladies. Can you help us?"

Even as dreams of a huge account lit up the woman's eyes, Becca protested. "Lady Roth, not for me! It is Emily who is to be presented."

"And will you not be accompanying her, my dear? And are you not a member of the family?"

Becca smiled at Lady Roth's arch questions. "Yes, my lady, but I am truly only the chaperon. A complete wardrobe is not necessary."

"Nonsense. If you are worried about Lucas, you must not. He will not cut up stiff over a few dress bills." She took Becca's hand and drew the young lady down to the chair beside her. "Besides, my dear, all the gowns in London could not repay the joy you have brought into our lives."

"I have done nothing, my lady," Becca protested. "It is you who have made me so welcome, treated me as one of the family." She fought back the tears that filled her eyes. "To take more from you would be too much."

Lady Roth patted her pale cheek. "You must not argue with me, my dear. You have become like a second daughter to me, and I want you to enjoy the Season also." With a conspiratorial wink at her own daughter, Lady Roth added, "I hope to celebrate the end of the Season with two weddings."

Emily nodded in agreement with her mother, a smile on her face. "Mama and I have decided to find you a husband, too, Becca. Then we will not have to worry about you finding another position when I have married. Mama is going to ask Lucas—"

"Emily, you must say nothing as yet." Her mother's firm tone stopped Emily's chattering and she looked guiltily at her parent.

"Allow me to enjoy choosing you a wardrobe, Becca, darling," Lady Roth went on. "After all, if it were not for you, I would be locked in my bedchamber, so protected by Lucas as to become addled."

With Madame Printemps waiting eagerly and the two dearest faces in the world to Becca pleading for her cooperation, she reluctantly nodded. But the thought of facing Lord Roth when he returned to Town was daunting.

Perhaps she could find a way to repay the cost of her wardrobe. She vowed she would repay her debt to Lord Roth when she gained control of her estate in six years, when she reached the advanced age of twenty-five, even if her trustees refused to advance her the sum at present.

Once Becca's agreement was secured, Madame Printemps became a veritable whirlwind, selecting styles and colours best suited to each young lady, her minions leaping to follow her rapid orders.

Becca was draped in hues that showed her dark

colouring to best advantage, though she attempted to keep Lady Roth's enthusiasm from overtaking her good judgement. Emily's daintiness was emphasized with the soft blues and pinks of the debutante. Both were beauties in their own way, and Madame Printemps was sure she would increase her business once it was known she had dressed two such lovely young ladies.

Becca dwelt happily on the thought of destroying her hated grey gowns immediately upon returning to Roth House. Madame Printemps had already completed a green sprigged muslin for another customer, and she offered it to Becca, who was delighted to discover that it fitted perfectly.

"And what shall we do weeth zis?" the Frenchwoman asked, holding up the grey garment Becca had worn into the shop.

With a swift glance at her employer, Becca said, "Anything you wish, *Madame*. I never want to see it again."

The other ladies joined in her laughter and the three of them left the shop, Lady Roth carried by Jem. From that day forth, their shopping trips were a delight to all three.

AS HE DROVE BACK into London two weeks later, Lord Roth encountered Sir Anthony, who invited him to take a turn in the Park in his new carriage.

"I have not yet even returned home, Tony. I am covered in dust."

"Nonsense, Lucas. You are never dishevelled. Besides, I need your opinion. I must decide whether to purchase this carriage."

Lord Roth debated the necessity of returning to Roth House at once and decided his mother would be resting and that Emily had her precious widow to keep watch over her. He had struggled to keep his sister's companion from his mind during his absence from London, but thoughts of her beauty sometimes intruded without warning.

Without more ado, he swung down from his own equipage, ordering his man to continue on without him, and joined Sir Anthony.

As the horses were set in motion, he leaned back and asked, "And what has been occurring in Town?"

"Nothing extraordinary. Poodle bought a new collar for his dog. Lady Jersey has a new flirt. Oh! I saw your cousin, the widow." He looked at his friend with a grin. "She is quite a beauty."

"She is not—that is, the connection is distant," Lord Roth snapped, his composure suddenly destroyed.

"Well, she is certainly attracting a lot of attention."

"I told my mother it would not do," Lord Roth muttered.

"Here, now," Sir Anthony said in alarm, "I did not mean to imply that she was beyond the pale. She and your sister make a charming pair."

"You've seen my sister?" He was surprised when his friend avoided his eye.

"Yes, shortly after you left Town. I paid a morning call on my godmother, Lady Abrams, and they were present."

"Did she behave herself?" Lord Roth asked, trying to discover why his friend would not meet his gaze.

Shocked, Tony turned to look at his friend. "Why, of course she did! Your sister was charming!"

"And the widow?"

"Mrs. Dunn behaved perfectly. My godmother was most pleased with both of them."

As they passed several acquaintances, acknowledging their greetings, Lord Roth drew a sigh of relief. "I was afraid Mrs. Dunn would not be suitable, but I could not dismiss her." Another thought occurred to him. "Was she wearing one of those awful grey gowns?"

"I do not remember noticing her gown, but it was fashionable. That much I do know. Both she and your sister were well turned out. Much as they are today."

"What? Today?" His friend's words recalled Lord Roth from his thoughts and his gaze followed his friend's gesture. Coming down the path towards them was his brougham, its top down to allow its occupants to see and be seen.

His eyes immediately sought out Rebecca Dunn. The charming young woman, her black curls artfully arranged, was clad in a green cloak and matching bonnet that made her eyes appear huge, her lips...

"Your mother seems quite well, too."

"Yes, she…my mother?" It was a physical effort for Lucas to force his eyes away from the widow, but Tony's words confounded him. He looked at his friend and then returned his gaze to the carriage. For the first time, he noted there were three women seated there. His sister, better turned out than he would have supposed, was seated across from Rebecca. Beside her was an older woman, her face aglow with health, a beaming smile on her lips.

Stunned, Lord Roth was scarcely aware of Tony halting his carriage. The ladies, however, noted his presence at once.

"Lucas, darling, when did you return?" Lady Roth asked in delight.

"Only today, Mama. I see you are well." His frown did not lead the other ladies to congratulate themselves on their care of Lady Roth.

"Oh, darling, I feel wonderful. And wait until you see the house. I have so much to tell you. Emily and Becca have worked so hard. And don't they look charming?"

Her direct appeal could not be ignored. He turned his gaze on the two younger ladies. "They appear to great advantage," he murmured.

"Shame on you, Lucas," Tony admonished. "They are diamonds of the first water, and well you know it. Ladies, you are a delight to the eyes."

Emily smiled demurely, her lashes fluttering over

pink cheeks. Becca smiled also, adding, "Thank you, Sir Anthony."

Lucas eyed his friend, a frown on his brow.

"We must move along," Lady Roth said, "but we shall see you at home for tea, Lucas. Sir Anthony, we would be most pleased to have you join us."

"I would never refuse an invitation from your lips, Lady Roth," he responded gallantly, before slapping the reins to continue on.

"MY BROTHER did not appear to be pleased, Mama. Do you think we did anything to upset him?"

"Why, Emily, darling, of course we did not," Lady Roth replied.

"I think he was surprised to see your mother out and about, Emily. I'm sure he could find nothing to complain of in your appearance. Certainly, Sir Anthony could not." Becca smiled as Emily's cheeks reddened.

"Sir Anthony was only being gallant," Emily assured her companions, but the other two exchanged conspiratorial smiles. They had encountered Lord Roth's friend several times in the past two weeks and had noticed his fascination with Emily's delicate beauty.

"Well, he will have more opportunities when he joins us for tea," Lady Roth said with satisfaction. "And Lucas will be amazed at all you have accomplished while he has been out of Town."

Becca hoped Lady Roth was correct, but the man's

reaction to his mother's presence had not been encouraging. Surely he could see the improvement in her health.

What had begun as an occasional outing had grown into a daily occurrence. Lady Roth, freed from her bedchamber, had taken delight in venturing out and meeting old friends. As a result of her activities, she was sleeping more soundly at night and her appetite had increased. Even more importantly, the sound of her laughter was heard with great frequency, lending an air of festivity to each day.

Or perhaps Lord Roth's unhappiness could be attributed to speculation about the money his mother had spent dressing her, a mere chaperon. Becca cringed at the thought. She hoped he would not complain to his mother because of it.

When they arrived home, Jem, now Lady Roth's personal footman, carried his precious burden up the front steps and into the foyer.

"Murdoch, Lord Roth and Sir Anthony will be joining us for tea in the parlour." Now that Lady Roth had emerged from the bedchamber, she had taken up the reins of the household once more.

"Yes, my lady. Lord Roth's carriage arrived over an hour ago. There have been many callers and several bouquets were delivered."

Lady Roth beamed at the two young ladies. "Aha! Your admirers are growing in number."

Becca nodded, smiling. "Emily has been quite well-received."

Nothing else was said until they were seated in the parlour, Lady Roth in the special chair Emily and Becca had had prepared for her. Plump cushions provided comfort and small wheels on each leg made it possible to move her about downstairs with little effort.

"It is not only Emily who has been well-received, Becca." Lady Roth allowed Emily to pour the tea that Murdoch had brought in.

Emily agreed with her mother. "That is correct. Mr. Bowden is in alt every time you appear, Becca. And Lord Castleberry follows you about as if he is afraid you will disappear." Her teasing smile showed no resentment that her chaperon shared in her success.

"You are exaggerating, Emily," Becca protested. In truth, she knew she attracted attention, but her situation was not improved by it. She had read enough to know that beauty alone would seldom tempt a man to marriage.

The secret knowledge that she had rank and wealth enough to find marriage without beauty should have been encouraging. But if she could not reveal her true identity, what did it matter? In spite of Emily's and Lady Roth's desire to see her wed, she did not think it possible. Her impetuosity had created a difficulty that she could not seem to resolve.

Lord Roth and Sir Anthony entered the room.

"Mother, should you not be resting after your outing?" Lord Roth questioned.

"Goodness, no, child. I am much stronger now.

Besides, these two tyrants will not allow me to over-tax myself.'' Her smile made it impossible for her son to insist that she retire.

Emily poured cups of tea for the gentlemen, and Sir Anthony hurried to take them from her, his eyes devouring her pretty face. ''Thank you, Lady Emily.''

''Sir Anthony, your new carriage is delightful,'' Becca said, giving Emily time to compose herself. The normally effervescent young lady was tongue-tied in the face of such admiration.

''Do you like it? I'm trying to decide whether to buy it.'' He turned to Emily. ''What is your opinion, Lady Emily?''

''It—it looked most comfortable, sir.''

''Would you care to ride in it tomorrow? Then you could assist me in my decision.'' He leaned forward, eager for her answer.

''I would enjoy it, if Mama agrees.'' Both young people turned to Lady Roth.

''Of course, my dears.''

''We have an appointment with Madame Printemps,'' Becca reminded Lady Roth.

''Ah.'' She looked at the downcast faces of Emily and Sir Anthony. ''I believe you and I shall go to *madame's* and allow Emily to accompany Sir Anthony.''

Everyone was pleased with her solution except her son. He stared at his mother. ''You cannot mean to visit Madame Printemps's salon, Mama. You must have her come here.''

"But, darling, it is so much simpler to go there. We have done so a number of times the past week. Haven't you noticed the girls' delightful gowns? Even I have ordered new gowns—they insisted I do so. It was so enjoyable!" Noticing her son's frown, she added with a laugh, "I promise we have not outrun our budget, dear."

Her son dismissed budgetary concerns with a wave of his hand. "I was concerned about your health, Mama, not bills. You look delightful today." He finally smiled, much to Becca's relief.

"You are not the only one to notice how pretty our mama is," Emily added, directing a teasing glance at her mother.

Lady Roth's delighted laughter surprised her son as much as his sister's words. "What do you mean?" he demanded.

"Do you remember Papa's particular friend, Mr. Ambrose?"

"Of course I do. His estate is near High Oaks. I occasionally see him."

"Well, he discovered Mama in the Park several days ago, and he has called on her every day since then."

"We have many friends in common and enjoy conversation," Lady Roth said simply, a smile on her lips.

Becca noted the consternation on Lord Roth's brow and decided a change of subject would be advisable.

"Lord Roth, do you approve of the new decoration

of the house?'' She waited until he turned to look at her before continuing. ''Emily has spent many hours, with your mother's guidance, redoing this room.''

''It is charming,'' he returned automatically, scarcely taking in the new blue draperies, the white-washed walls, the petit-point sofa and soft rose chairs grouped around the tea table. His mind still dwelt on his mother and the changes that had taken place in his absence. ''I believe you should see a doctor, Mama,'' he said abruptly, dismissing decoration as a subject for discussion.

''A doctor? But I am perfectly well, dear. Oh, and wait until you see the dining-room. Emily and Becca have improved it so much. I cannot wait until we give a dinner party. They discovered a wonderful new centre-piece that is so elegant.''

Before he could turn the subject back to her health, the door opened and Murdoch led in several callers, including Mr. Ambrose. The next hour was spent in general conversation. Lord Roth watched as his wom-enfolk became the centre of attention.

In truth, he was in a state of confusion. When he'd thought of bringing his sister to London for the Sea-son, he had merely intended to hire someone to escort her about, find her a husband and marry her off. Then he and his mother would return to High Oaks and carry on as before. But now he realized that nothing would ever be the same again.

While he was glad his mother was happy, he couldn't help being concerned about her health. And it appeared his house would be overrun with admirers of his mother as well as of his sister.

And then there was Becca—Mrs. Dunn, he reminded himself. He could not deny that several of the callers were her admirers. Not that he blamed them; she was enchanting. He wondered if Emily were bothered by Becca's success, as he'd feared. But careful inspection of his sister uncovered no signs of resentment, only an enjoyment of her tea and the congenial company.

LORD ROTH SUMMONED Dr. Browning, one of the physicians to the Prince Regent himself, the very next morning. He wanted to ensure that his mother not ruin her health by all her exertions.

Lady Roth was on her *chaise longue* conferring with Becca when he arrived. At his knock, Becca opened the door, and he stared at her beautiful face in surprise.

"Becca! I mean, Mrs. Dunn. I did not know you were with my mother."

"Yes, my lord. Did you wish to speak with her?"

"Er, yes. I have brought Dr. Browning to examine her."

Becca turned back into the room, leaving the door open. "My lady, Lord Roth is here and has brought a doctor to examine you."

Lady Roth sighed. "Very well. Allow them to come in."

The two gentlemen entered and Lord Roth introduced the doctor to the two ladies.

"Your son has expressed concern about your activities, my lady. May I examine you?" The doctor was already studying his new patient.

"Yes, of course, if it will please Lucas. But I am in excellent health, sir."

"Mama, it is just a precaution."

"Very well, Lucas, I understand."

He turned to leave, but noted that Becca intended to remain. "Shall we leave, Mrs. Dunn?"

"I thought I might stay to assist the doctor, my lord." Becca smiled at Lady Roth for approval. Even though Lady Roth's maid was in attendance, Becca thought she would prefer her to stay.

"Yes. I think I would like Becca to remain with us. You do not mind, Dr. Browning?"

"Not at all, my lady. She will make a charming assistant."

Left with no choice, Lord Roth found himself in the hall, excluded from his mother's bedchamber. "Even the doctor is taken with her, blast him! I suppose next he will suggest she come to work for him." he muttered to himself as he descended to the library, determined to catch up on the paperwork he had neglected for the past two weeks.

"Murdoch, I shall be in the library. Please ask the doctor to attend me there when he has completed his examination."

Murdoch, surrounded by flowers that had recently

been delivered, acknowledged his employer's order in a distracted fashion.

"What are all these?" Lord Roth demanded as he noted the numerous bouquets.

"Offerings for our young ladies, my lord," Murdoch said with obvious pride.

With a disgusted growl, Lord Roth retreated to the library. How was a man supposed to have peace with all the goings-on about the place? he wondered.

A short time later, Murdoch escorted Dr. Browning into the room. With a smile, the man took the seat across from his host, refusing his offer of a drink.

"I have more patients to visit this morning. I must not appear to have partaken of spirits," he told him.

"My mother?" Lord Roth asked, in no mood for social niceties.

"In excellent health. She tells me the accident occurred two years ago, and since then, until recently, she has kept to her bed."

"I thought it best."

Looking under lowered lids at the young man across from him, Dr. Browning chose his words carefully. "The excellent care you gave your mother has allowed her to recuperate amazingly well. Her recent activity has improved her health only because she had such good early care." His patient abovestairs had warned him not to hurt her son's feelings.

"So she is not damaging her health by all this larking about?"

"On the contrary, my lord. I think it has benefited

her. In fact, I detected some movement in her lower limbs.''

After staring at the doctor, Lord Roth downed in one swallow the glass of sherry he had poured for himself. Huskily, he asked, ''Do you mean to say my mother can walk?''

CHAPTER FOUR

"No, my lord," the doctor replied hurriedly. "Nor do I promise she will ever walk in the future. I am no fortune-teller." He cleared his throat. "However, I believe it is possible that she may recover to some extent."

Myriad feelings swarmed in Lord Roth's head: joy, relief, guilt, jealousy. *He* had wanted to give his mother the world, and a beautiful stranger had forestalled him.

"I can also assure you that her present activities do her no harm," the doctor added. When he perceived that Lord Roth was preoccupied with thoughts of his own, he stood. "I'll be on my way if you have no other questions, my lord. My patients are awaiting me."

"Of course," Lucas agreed absently, standing also. "You will make regular visits? I do not want my mother to overtax herself."

"Of course."

Lord Roth ascended to his mother's chamber as soon as the doctor left. She was chattering to Mrs. Dunn as Eva answered his knock.

"Come in, my lord," Becca said as he hesitated

on the threshold. "I'm sure you want to visit with your mother. If you will excuse me, my lady, I shall see if Emily has need of me."

He watched as the beautiful widow slipped from the room.

"Did you talk with Dr. Browning?" His mother's words recalled his attention.

"Yes, Mama. And I am delighted with his news," he assured her.

"Thank you, darling. It is due only to your good care of me these past two years. I cannot believe it!"

With painful honesty, Lord Roth added, "And the happiness Mrs. Dunn has brought you."

Lady Roth extended her hand to her son. "Child, you have always brought me happiness as well. Let us cry quits on who is responsible."

"Very well. Tell me if I may do aught to hasten your recovery."

"Lucas, dear, I…you may not like what I am about to request, but Becca has given so much to me, to Emily, that I would like to give her something in return. And she *is* part of the family."

"A gift would certainly be appropriate. What have you in mind, Mama?"

"A husband."

Lucas choked. "I beg your pardon?"

"Oh, not as a gift, but I wish to make it possible for her to—to find happiness. After Emily marries, Becca's position will not exist. Of course, I could keep her as my companion, but I am not certain she would accept.''

"Mama, what do you mean? How do you propose to provide Becca with a husband if it is not of her choosing?''

"I don't mean to force a husband on her, but if you were to provide her with a dowry—nothing large, just a decent portion—then she would receive offers, I am sure.''

"So am I," Lord Roth muttered, his heart sinking at his mother's suggestion. He did not look forward to receiving offers for Becca's hand.

His mother looked anxiously at her son's face. "Dear, if you do not care for the idea, I can use some of the funds your father left me. Do not concern yourself." Something was upsetting him, and yet she did not think it was the sum of money. Lucas had never been selfish.

"No, Mama, do not be ridiculous," he said, bending low to kiss her cheek. "Of course we must provide for Becca. After all, she has given us a gift out of all proportion to your request. And as head of the family, it is entirely proper for me to provide for one of our members. I shall see my man of business at once."

"Lucas, I have been blessed in my children," his mother said, beaming up at him. "You are such a dear."

"Nonsense, Mama," he said, squeezing her hand. "It is I who am blessed."

When he rose to leave the room, she clung to his hand. "Why not inform Becca of her good fortune now? Will you send for the girls?"

Lucas stared at his parent, wondering how he could escape such a scene. But, of course, there was no way out, not when it was what his mother wanted. With an abrupt nod, he crossed to the bell-pull. Upon Eva's appearance, he commanded the presence of Lady Emily and Mrs. Dunn.

When the two young ladies entered the room a few minutes later, they discovered Lady Roth and her son casually talking about events in Society.

"Mama, Becca has told me the good news! I am so thrilled."

"As I am, my dear. I shall not be able to dance at your ball, but someday, perhaps, I shall dance again."

Becca stood to one side as Emily embraced her mother. She felt ill at ease in Lord Roth's presence. Perhaps it was the powerful attraction she felt towards the man, or the reserve he exhibited whenever she drew close. She only knew she could not relax when he was near.

"Becca, you must come to me," Lady Roth commanded, a wide smile on her face.

Obediently, Becca moved to the bedside, taking the hand Lady Roth extended. "Yes, my lady?"

"Child, you have become like a precious second daughter to me, and a sister to Emily."

"Thank you, my lady, but it is your graciousness, yours and Emily's, which has made me so welcome."

Lady Roth only smiled. "I do not want to talk of payment for what you have done for us," she said, smiling again at Becca's quick shake of her head. "But I wish to ensure your future. It is a small thing to do in return for your gift to me."

"Please, my lady, I have done nothing."

"Ssh, my dear. When Emily marries, she will no longer need a chaperon. I shall, of course, always welcome you to my home, but I have already recognized your stubborn independence."

Lord Roth watched as Becca's cheeks flushed. She had never looked more lovely. His stomach tightened with longing, even as he stepped forward to set in motion what would ensure her marriage to another.

"My mother wishes to provide a dowry for you, Mrs. Dunn, so that you may also find a husband this Season." He hoped to speed up the interview so he might remove himself from the woman's presence.

Wide green eyes stared at him as first shock and then comprehension filled their depths.

"No! Oh, no, my lady, please, that is not necessary!"

"Becca, darling, Lucas has blurted out my plan, but he has the right of it. With your beauty, your gentility, it is only the lack of a dowry that would keep you from finding happiness. You have given it to us, and it is only right that we return that happiness to you."

Becca pulled her hand free and backed away from the trio of Roths. "I cannot accept such a—a gift. I do not seek a husband, my lady. Do not concern your-self with my future.'' Her words ended with a sob and she ran from the room.

In the stunned silence following, Emily said, ''Why is she disturbed? I thought she would be happy.''

''Do not worry, child. She will agree to our gift when she has considered it. I believe she did not ex-pect such kindness,'' Lady Roth replied.

''Or perhaps she is afraid of marriage. Maybe her husband was so cruel to her that she cannot bear the thought of marrying again,'' Emily said, her eyes lighting up in speculation.

Lucas's heart cringed at such a thought, but he of-fered another that was almost as painful. ''Or perhaps she loved her husband so well that she cannot bear another to take his place.''

''Whatever the reason,'' Lady Roth said kindly, ''I will convince her to plan for her future. And you, young lady, where did you hear of such a marriage as you described?''

Before Emily could think of an answer to conceal the fact that she had secretly been reading romantic novels, Lord Roth excused himself. He wanted to re-turn to the more mundane world of estate business. It, at least, did not twist his insides into knots.

BECCA THREW HERSELF across the bed as silent tears slipped down her cheeks. Such kindness as shown by Lady Roth was beyond anything, particularly in the face of her lies. What should she do?

In the several weeks she'd spent at Roth House, Becca had felt happier than she had since her father's death changed her life forever. She had not looked beyond the Season, determined to enjoy the life she was leading at present.

But Lady Roth's generosity forced her to consider her future. She could not accept a proposal without revealing her true identity, and when she did so, she feared the ton would reject her for her lies. Even if they did not, for they were generally tolerant of anyone with wealth, she would feel the dishonour.

She *could* remain silent, keeping her identity forever hidden…unless her aunt and uncle came to London. Becca sat up in bed, her fists clenched. But why should she give up her fortune, her estates? If she remained unmarried for six more years, according to her father's will, she could set up house and control her own destiny. Her people, those living on her estates, were depending on her.

Surely Lady Roth and Lady Emily would forgive her deception when they learned the truth of it. She would not have to sacrifice their friendship. Lord Roth's visage swam before her eyes. She feared he would not be as forgiving.

She straightened her shoulders and raised her chin, her decision made. Until the Season ended, she would remain at Roth House and refuse all offers. Then she would owe Lord Roth nothing, because there would be no need for a dowry.

When Lady Emily married, she would find another

position, and another and another, until she gained control of her fortune. At least she had independence to look forward to.

Jumping up from the bed, she hurried over to the table and poured cold water into the basin. A quick wash of her face erased the traces of tears. After smoothing her hair, she stepped out into the hall.

"Oh, Maisie," she called to the tweeny, "has Lord Roth left her ladyship's chamber?"

"Yes, Mrs. Dunn."

Thank goodness. She had no desire to face those penetrating blue eyes again so soon after her emotional display.

Lady Roth bade her enter when she knocked on the door, and she slipped into the room to join Lady Emily at her mother's bedside.

"My lady, please forgive my behaviour. Your generosity overwhelmed me, but that is no excuse for my poor manners."

"Nonsense, child," Lady Roth said, extending a hand. There was a warm smile on her face, but her blue eyes, so like her son's, studied Becca intently.

"But, Becca, why—" Emily began, but her mother cut short her question.

"Emily, dear, I believe you should lie down before dressing for the ball this evening. We are attending Lady Henderson's, are we not? I'm sure it will be a shocking crush."

"But, Mama, I—"

"Emily." The quietly spoken rebuke had its effect.

"Very well. I shall go and lie down." As the young lady walked past Becca, she cast her a look of such command that Becca was left in no doubt that her presence in Lady Emily's chamber was necessary immediately after she left Lady Roth.

As soon as the door closed behind her daughter, Lady Roth patted the side of the bed. "Sit here, Becca. I want to talk to you."

Though she followed her employer's orders, Becca carefully kept her gaze lowered to her hands, which were folded in her lap.

"Dear child, I had no intention of distressing you. I wanted only to provide for you, as if you were my own."

Becca said nothing, but nodded her head to show she understood.

"In truth, you should complain that you are not receiving a dowry like Emily's."

"Oh, no, my lady, of course not! You are being more than generous as it is." Her gaze rose with her protest to stare at her benefactress.

"Ah, at least you will now look at me." She smiled at Becca's blush. "Child, we are blessed in our wealth, more than is good for us, probably. What we share with you will not cause us discomfort. Please say you will accept so little."

Grateful that she'd resolved her future in her own mind, Becca smiled warmly at Lady Roth. "My lady, should I marry while in your employment, I shall accept the dowry you have so graciously offered."

"Wonderful. What an exciting Season we have ahead of us, with the two most beautiful young ladies in Society." Lady Roth leaned back on her pillow, a delightful smile on her face. "Tell me, darling Becca, in the week we have been attending balls, have you seen anyone to your liking?"

Becca silently cursed the flames that rose in her cheeks as Lord Roth's face flashed before her. "No, my lady," she lied. "I truly do not seek a second marriage."

"Very well, child. Do not concern yourself. There is plenty of time." She paused before adding, "Could you bring yourself to address me as Aunt Catherine?"

"Of course, my lady—Aunt Catherine—if that is your wish. I would be honoured to do so."

"We are relations, child. I should like it."

Becca nodded and stood, asking to be excused. As she left the room, Lady Roth's eyes narrowed. In spite of Becca's agreement, she knew the girl was not being completely honest. A mother's instinct told her the young lady was well on her way to being in love with someone. The only question was, with whom?

BY THE TIME Lord Roth strolled into his club later in the day, he had formulated a plan to escape the problems of his household. He would invite Tony and one or two other friends to his hunting lodge for several weeks.

As long as he returned in time for Emily's come-out ball, three weeks away, he knew his mother would excuse him. In fact, the trio of women seemed to go on so well without him, they probably would not even miss him. He did not want to consider why that thought disturbed him.

"Roth, over here, man," Tony called from a corner of the reading room, raising the eyebrows of those who'd sought peace from the noise of the gaming rooms.

Lord Roth strolled over to join Sir Anthony and several other friends. Just as he was about to launch into his invitation, Sir Anthony eagerly demanded, "What entertainment shall we attend this evening?"

"I say, Tony," Lord Deveril drawled. "You sound as though you are looking forward to it."

Though his flushed cheeks betrayed him, Tony tried for nonchalance. "Of course not, but I thought, as Lucas's friends, we should show support for his sister. After all, Dev, when your sister was fired off, we made sure her dance card was always full."

"My sister wasn't a diamond of the first water like Lady Emily. Girl doesn't need our help. We'd probably be trampled in the rush." He paused to cast a sly look at Lord Roth before murmuring, "Especially if she is accompanied by Mrs. Dunn."

Lucas avoided all eyes. He had hoped to escape from thoughts of the woman, but it seemed he could not.

"Tell us, Lucas, is the lady well provided for?" Mr. Whitechurch asked.

"Do you speak of my sister?"

Surprised by the coolness of his friend's tone, Mr. Whitechurch said, "I was not slighting your sister, Lucas. Everyone knows Lady Emily has a fortune."

Lord Roth could not hold back a sigh. "I did not mean to offend. I find myself ill-suited to Town life. In fact—"

"But you must supervise Lady Emily's Season," Sir Anthony insisted.

"I am sure the ladies are quite—"

"Heard there are several wastrels in Town looking to repair their fortunes," Lord Deveril said, interrupting Lucas's protest. "I'm glad m'sister's already settled. Some of those gamesters can be devilishly charming to the ladies."

Lucas's heart sank. His friends had the right of it, of course. Escape had only been a fleeting hope. He could not abandon his sister, or Mrs. Dunn, to such wolves.

"You never answered my question regarding the Dunn beauty, Lucas," Mr. Whitechurch complained.

Though every instinct counselled denial, Lord Roth complied with his friend's request.

"Mrs. Dunn has a dowry of...of five thousand pounds. Small, but sufficient when combined with her personal charms, I believe."

"But she is Lady Emily's chaperon, is she not?" Lord Deveril asked, a frown on his brow.

"Yes, but she is a distant family connection, and my mother would be well pleased were Mrs. Dunn happily settled."

"We will ensure it is known," Mr. Whitechurch told his friend, happy to serve him.

"Well, Lady Roth has no cause for worry. Neither lady will be left on the shelf, that much is certain," Lord Deveril said, leaning back in his chair.

That was a fact that only increased Lord Roth's malaise.

BECCA LEFT HER ROOM that evening dressed for the Henderson ball in a foam green silk overskirt and bodice, trimmed with Alenọn lace that matched the white underskirt. Green slippers peeked out from beneath her gown and white roses decorated her dark curls.

She had already been to Lady Emily's room several times to check on her charge, but she stopped at her door again. "Emily, are you ready to descend?"

The maid swung open the door and Becca smiled. Emily's blond beauty was accented by a pale blue gown that emphasized her exquisite form.

"Oh, my, many hearts will break tonight."

Emily smiled in delight but returned the compliment. "Only half of them will be laid at my door, Becca. You will drive them to distraction."

Well pleased with themselves, the two young ladies went down to dinner. Becca had decided that while she had no intention of accepting any proposals, she had every intention of enjoying the only Season she might ever experience.

"Is Mr. Ambrose going to escort us this evening?" Emily asked as they went down the stairs.

"I do not know. Your mother did not say who would be our escort. In truth, I suppose we may manage on our own."

"But it is more comfortable to have a man accompany us, even if he *is* my mother's admirer," Emily added with a giggle.

Better Mr. Ambrose than Lord Roth, Becca decided. Along with her other decisions about the Season, she had vowed to avoid Emily's brother, so that she might put from her mind the attraction she felt there. Since he had shown little interest in his sister's debut, she felt confident in her plans.

When they entered the parlour, Emily's question about their escort was immediately answered, and Becca's confidence crumbled.

CHAPTER FIVE

"GOOD EVENING, LADIES," Lord Roth murmured as both he and Sir Anthony bowed.

"Is this not charming?" Lady Roth said brightly. "These gentlemen have offered to be our escorts for the evening."

Lady Emily's smile was directed at Sir Anthony and expressed her appreciation. Becca took one look at Lord Roth and felt her heart sink. Evening clothes enhanced his blond handsomeness, making it impossible to ignore the tug on her heart.

"Lucas, ring for Murdoch. We must dine speedily if we are not to arrive too late this evening. Lady Henderson is sure to have a good turnout."

Lord Roth pushed his mother in to dinner in her special chair, followed by Sir Anthony, who gallantly extended an arm to each young lady.

"Lucas and I shall be the envy of all the young bucks this evening," Sir Anthony said after they were all seated. "You will save a dance for us, will you not?"

Though his question was directed to both ladies, Lady Emily's blush had nothing to do with the prospect of a dance with her brother.

Becca sat frozen in dismay. She had not thought that she might dance with Lord Roth. With her hands tightly clasped in her lap, she murmured, "I believe, as chaperon, I should not dance."

"Nonsense, child." Lady Roth arched her eyebrows. "Do you not remember our earlier discussion? You *must* dance."

"Indeed, Mrs. Dunn, I personally know several gallants who would be severely disappointed if you did not dance with them."

Sir Anthony's teasing relaxed the tension building in Becca, but she did not dare look at Lord Roth. "I shall do whatever Lady Roth wishes."

"Good. Then I wish that Sir Anthony dance with you and Lucas with his sister the first dance. Then you may exchange partners, before surrendering yourselves to the crush. I want everyone to know that you as well as Emily are under Lucas's care."

A footman entered with the first course, and Lady Roth, whose appetite was now normal, turned her attention to the turtle soup.

Becca sat paralyzed by thoughts of dancing with Lord Roth. At least the second dance was not likely to be a waltz, as waltzes were usually played later in the evening.

"Have you no appetite, Mrs. Dunn?"

Becca's green gaze lifted to her host and her breath grew shallow. "Of course, my lord. I was just... anticipating the delights of the evening before us."

"As am I," he muttered, but Becca saw a strange light in his eyes that she could not interpret. It was almost as if he were flirting with her, but such a thought was absurd.

LORD ROTH SWUNG his sister around him even as his eyes followed his friend and Becca. Mrs. Dunn's graceful beauty was attracting many masculine eyes. He wished he could spirit her away from those who would pursue her. Instead, he must stand aside.

But he would have one dance.

As the music ended, he led Emily back to his mother, comfortably seated among the dowagers. As he had expected, by the time his sister and Becca reached the edge of the dance floor, there were a number of gentlemen waiting for introductions. Obviously Whitechurch and Dev had spread the word about Becca's dowry.

He and Lord Anthony performed the introductions and watched the young ladies' dance cards fill. Before the musicians had struck up the first dance, they had already been assured of never having to be wallflowers. Even the waltzes, which Lady Emily was not permitted to dance, were filled on her card. Many gentlemen preferred sitting out a dance in her company to being a partner to some lesser beauty.

As a widow, Becca could, of course, dance the waltz, and Lord Roth stopped a footman for a whispered conference. There was a discreet exchange and then he stood back and allowed access to the lovely widow. Yes, he would have his one dance.

BECCA WAS FLUSTERED by the gentlemen's pleas for dances. She had been well-received from the beginning, but there was a difference this evening. Could word have already circulated about the proposed dowry? Were men so intent on lining their pockets that their feelings did not matter?

Attempting to hide her dismay, Becca smiled, but her smile lacked its normal radiance. If men were so mercenary, it was as well she had determined to remain independent.

Much to her surprise, she was relieved when the musicians struck up the second dance and she could escape with Lord Roth. At least *he* did not seek her out for her dowry. Therefore, her smile brightened as he appeared at her side.

He led her to the floor just as the orchestra leader noted a change in the program. "Ladies and gentlemen, we shall now play a waltz."

Lord Roth slipped his gloved hand around her waist and she stared up at him in surprise. "A waltz? My lord, I do not…that is, Emily has shown me the steps but—"

"It is a simple dance, my dear. Just relax and I shall guide you."

His calm voice instilled a confidence that surprised her. After several minutes, she truly did relax as she realized her partner was an excellent teacher.

"You are enjoying yourself?"

Her green-eyed gaze lifted to his face briefly before she returned her eyes to his white cravat. "Yes, my lord."

They took several more turns about the room before he spoke again. "You certainly have no lack of partners."

The warmth of his hand at her waist, his closeness, almost distracted her from his remarks. She remained silent.

"Is there something the matter?"

"No, of course not, my lord."

"But you did not answer. And no one can hear us. There is no need to be formal at the moment. When we are alone or among family, I believe it proper for you to call me Lucas. After all, we are relations."

"I did not hear a question, L-Lucas," Becca replied. "I-I must have been concentrating on the steps," she said in an effort to disguise her embarrassment, for she had in fact been thinking of the warmth of his arm about her waist.

"Very well. Are you not pleased to be surrounded by so many eager gentlemen?"

Once again she looked at him, only to turn her eyes away. "Perhaps, if I thought they were clamouring for my attention because of my own merits and not for a dowry that has suddenly been bestowed upon me."

He pulled her closer, causing her to stumble slightly.

"My apologies," he murmured as he relaxed his hold on her. "You must not try to reform Society. Even the Nonconformists have given up on us and turned to saving the lower ranks."

Becca stumbled again. She needed no instructions on the Nonconformists. Her aunt and uncle were firm believers. "And shall you select your bride by her dowry?" she dared ask, her gaze firmly fixed on his face.

He said nothing as he swung her round, her gown flowing out in a graceful arc.

"Lucas?" she prompted.

"I have no need of another fortune, since my father was beforehand with the world, Becca, though I would not refuse a dowry."

Becca had no response, but her smile disappeared and her enjoyment of the evening went with it.

LORD ROTH HAD NO INTEREST in finding another partner after his waltz with Becca. However, the ever-alert Lady Henderson enlisted his and Sir Anthony's efforts in rescuing lonely wallflowers. But in spite of his activities, he managed to keep the lovely widow in sight during most of the evening.

One of her partners, an older, more sophisticated man than the others, brought several blushes to Becca's cheeks, he noted. The sight caused his Lordship to squeeze his partner's hand so tightly, she gasped.

"I beg your pardon," he said quickly, glancing

down at the shy young lady. "I hope I did not hurt you?"

"No, my lord. Of course not."

In spite of the expectancy in her eyes, Lord Roth's partner received no more of his attention as the music ended. His own eyes were on Becca.

With a nonchalance contradicted by his intent gaze, he wandered over to Becca's former partner, who was now leaning against a pillar chatting with friends.

"Evening, Chancelor," he said, nodding to the others. "Enjoying yourself?"

"Tolerably, Roth, tolerably. Beauty is definitely present this evening."

"You are referring to Mrs. Dunn, my sister's chaperon, who is also a member of our family?" His tone challenged the man to take care.

"You cannot deny her beauty, Roth," he returned.

"No, nor can you deny my responsibility, as head of our family, to protect her."

The man's brows rose. "I have done nothing to arouse your protective instincts, Roth. I only danced with the lady. In fact, she refused my invitation to drive in the Park on the morrow."

While inwardly he cheered Becca's decision, Lord Roth kept his features stern. "Perhaps that is because you overstepped the mark."

"I did no such thing." Under Lucas's challenging stare, he muttered, "Perhaps some of my comments were a little warm, but she is a widow, not an innocent virgin."

Several others nodded their heads, as if in agreement with Chancelor's remarks. Lord Roth had no such tolerance, however. "Mrs. Dunn is to be treated with the respect due a gentlewoman, Chancelor. I shall demand no less."

His cold words were met with surprised silence and not a little fear. After all, he had a reputation as an excellent marksman, and his bouts with Gentleman Jackson were well attended.

"Here now, Roth, I meant no harm," Chancelor said quickly, holding up his hands. "There are plenty of other widows available."

Lord Roth noted the stares from those near him and nodded, turning away without another word. He did not want to call further attention to himself.

Tony was waiting and fell into step with him as he walked around the ballroom. "What was the cause of that commotion?"

"What? Nothing. You are enjoying yourself?"

His friend studied him carefully before saying, "Yes, of course. I am taking Lady Emily in to supper. Shall you and Mrs. Dunn join us?"

"Damn! I forgot to write in my name," he muttered. "I shall see if she is available."

Laughing, Tony assured him, "You will not have the opportunity. They are buzzing around the two of them thicker than bees at a honey-pot."

"Then I shall adjourn to the card room, lest Lady Henderson present me with some unfortunate young lady who has not found a partner."

He remained in the card room until the final dance, unwilling to observe Becca's social triumphs. However, good manners dictated that as escort to the Ladies Roth as well as to Mrs. Dunn, he present himself in the ballroom for the finale.

Becca spun round the room one last time, appearing as fresh as she had at the beginning of the evening. Lord Roth's thoughts lingered on his own dance with her, when he had held her in his arms, the lilac scent she always wore swirling about them.

A hand on his shoulder shook him from his reverie.

"I am ready for this evening to end, Lucas. It is not pleasant watching friends become giddy because of certain young ladies." Tony's face was unusually grim.

"To whom do you refer?"

"There are too many to name. Lady Emily has only to smile and they are pledging their allegiance to her. Mrs. Dunn, too, has many admirers, but she doesn't encourage them as much."

"Do you mean to say my sister is a flirt?"

"No! Of course not," Tony protested, his cheeks flaming. "It is only...Lady Emily is less experienced."

"Never mind, my friend. The ball is at an end. Let us go collect the ladies and escape this madhouse."

THOUGH LADY ROTH had withstood the rigours of the evening remarkably well, once they were seated in the carriage, she laid her head on Becca's shoulder and fell asleep. Lady Emily, though she kept her voice low so as not to disturb her mother, chattered about the evening.

"Becca, did you meet Mr. Gardine? He particularly wished to talk to you, but when next I saw you, he was not there."

"I believe I did meet him," Becca said quietly. In truth, the evening had not been delightful. She had grown weary of the gentlemen and the dancing very early on—shortly after her dance with Lord Roth, in fact.

"I'm sure it would be hard to remember. We met so many gentlemen this evening, and they were all so attentive."

Even from across the coach, Becca could sense that Sir Anthony had stiffened. With a slight warning in her voice she said, "Yes, we were both most fortunate. However, I find it more enjoyable to spend time with those I know."

"Well, yes, of course, but it is delightful to make new friends," Emily returned, a reminiscent smile on her lips.

Sir Anthony snorted in a most ungentlemanly fashion, drawing Emily's attention. "You do not care to make friends, Sir Anthony?"

"Friends? Yes, indeed, Lady Emily, I enjoy making friends. I do not believe I have ever danced with a *friend*, however." His sarcastic tone wiped the smile from Lady Emily's face.

"Then it is clear I am not to consider you a friend,

sir," she replied stiffly, and turned her face to stare out the window of the coach.

Unhappiness replaced Lady Emily's earlier gaiety and nothing more was said until Roth House was reached. The two men descended and turned to assist the young ladies. Lady Emily ignored Sir Anthony and allowed her brother to hand her down. Sir Anthony offered his services to Becca, which did not appear to please Emily.

After Lord Roth had scooped up his mother, the party entered the brightly lit entry hall.

Becca looked at Emily's rigid features and turned to the two gentlemen. "Thank you for your escort this evening, gentlemen. We are fatigued and will retire now." She took Emily's arm and led the way up the stairs. Though Emily said nothing, she turned to stare at Sir Anthony with sad eyes before disappearing down the hall.

"We are home?" Lady Roth asked her son drowsily.

"Yes, Mama, we are home. I'll have you to your bed at once." As he turned to go up the stairs, he said, "Will you wait, Tony? I shall only be a minute and then I'll offer you the hospitality of the house."

Tony nodded and Lucas asked Murdoch to show his friend to the library. He joined him there several minutes later.

"Lord, to think females delight in such functions for an entire Season," he said as he entered. "I don't think I can bear many more."

"There will be no point in my doing so," Tony replied gloomily.

"What do you mean?"

"Lady Emily will never dance with me again."

Lucas filled two glasses with brandy and handed one to his friend before sitting down across from him. "Come now, Tony, do not be ridiculous. Emily will not even remember what was said on the morrow. And if she does, send her a bouquet of flowers and a pretty apology."

As he leaned back in his chair to sip the brandy, Lord Roth was struck by the anguish on his friend's face. It suddenly occurred to him that Tony was expressing uncommon concern that his sister might be upset.

Sitting up, he asked, "Tony, you are not...you do not...that is, surely you are not trying to fix your interest with *Emily?*"

Sir Anthony turned beet red. "I—I...why ever not? She is beautiful, and enchanting, and graceful—"

"Enough, friend," Lucas said, holding up his hand.

"You object?" he asked anxiously.

Lucas rose to place a hand on Tony's shoulder. "Of course not. You are my friend. I would delight in welcoming you into my family...if you are sure of your feelings."

"I was sure when I first met her at High Oaks. She was only sixteen and already a beauty. I have been waiting for her arrival in London ever since."

Lord Roth stared at his friend in amazement. "Then I am happy for you."

Tony downed his glass of brandy and stood. "But *she* is unhappy with me. What if she will not speak to me?"

"Apologize, as I said. Women enjoy our begging for forgiveness."

"Yes, yes, I'll send flowers at once. And I'll write a note, saying all that is proper, of course," he assured his friend.

"I had no doubt. Are your intentions—that is, shall you offer for her? Am I to speak to her of your interest?" Lucas asked, unsure exactly what his friend meant.

"No! Not yet. I must be sure she cares for me. I mean, I know I am a good catch, Lucas, but I want— I want her heart as well as her hand." Tony stared across the room, a smile on his face that left Lucas feeling lonely.

"Very well. I will say nothing."

Tony spun round. "Well, it wouldn't hurt if you put in a good word for me."

"Done, whether you asked or not."

"Thank you, Lucas. You are a true friend." Tony shook his hand and then wandered to the door, a distracted look on his face.

"Are you leaving now?"

"What? Oh, yes, yes, I had best be on my way. I must write that note, you know." With a wave of his hand, Tony strolled out of the room.

Lucas stared after him for several minutes before he turned to the decanter and refilled his glass. What an unexpected turn. He'd feared no one would see Emily as long as Becca was beside her.

But Emily, little Emily, had caught Tony. He saluted his sister with his glass before taking a sip. As soon as Tony came to the sticking point and offered for her, the Season would be over for the Roths.

That, of course, was what he wanted, but the question of Becca's future remained. To be sure, there was time for any number of offers. And if the throng of men surrounding her tonight was any indication, there would be a parade of them in the not too distant future.

He drank the last of the brandy in his glass and considered filling it again. He was blue-devilled for some reason this evening. But he had learned his lesson concerning the after-effects of overindulgence in his salad days.

With a sigh, he struggled from his chair and followed Tony's path to the front hall. With a good-night to Murdoch, he climbed the stairs, lifting each foot as if it were weighted down with rocks.

At the top of the stairs, as he was about to turn in the opposite direction from the ladies' chambers, he caught a flash of white in the candlelight.

"Mrs. Dunn?" he called in surprise.

"Yes, my lord," came the whispered response.

"Is all well?"

Though he could not distinguish her features in the dim light, he saw her reassure him with a nod.

"Then why are you strolling about at this late hour?"

"I just wanted to look in on your mother, now that I have settled Emily. She...she was a little upset."

"Ah." Lord Roth spoke on impulse, though his instincts told him to avoid the lady. "I think, Becca, that you and I must have a chat."

CHAPTER SIX

"Now, my lord?" Becca asked incredulously. Surely the man did not mean to discuss anything when dawn was almost breaking.

He stepped back and shook his head. "Of course not. I meant in the morning. We shall have our talk in the morning."

Before she could reply, he had spun on his heel and disappeared down the shadowy hallway as if pursued. Becca stood there, staring after him, her thoughts all ajumble.

Sighing, she turned and walked to her bedchamber, the candle in her hand flickering. She was exhausted. Emily had been upset with Sir Anthony and had wanted to complain to Becca. It had taken almost an hour to settle her down to sleep.

In spite of her curiosity about the talk Lord Roth wanted to have with her, Becca fell asleep as soon as her head reached the pillow. But it was her first waking thought the next day.

Since it was almost twelve of the clock, Becca dressed hurriedly, selecting a simple yellow morning gown and pulling her hair back in an uncomplicated style. She rushed to the breakfast room, hoping to settle her nerves with a cup of tea before she faced the master of the house.

"Good morning, Murdoch. Has Lord Roth come down yet?"

"No, madam. May I serve you?"

Becca collapsed on her chair with a sigh of relief. "Oh, thank you, Murdoch." Now she could enjoy her breakfast.

She was lingering over a second cup of tea when Lady Roth entered the breakfast room, carried by Jem.

"Aunt Catherine!" Becca exclaimed, jumping to her feet to pull out her chair. "Surely you should not be up and about so early after our late night."

"More likely I than you, child," the older lady said with a laugh. "At least I take little naps. You have been run off your feet." She paused to thank the butler as he poured her a cup of tea and filled her plate.

Once he had withdrawn, she continued, "You must tell me if we demand too much of you, Becca."

"Not at all, Aunt, I am enjoying a life of leisure," Becca assured her with a laugh.

"Ah, then Emily did not talk your ear off after the ball?"

Becca avoided her eyes. "We talked over the entertainment, of course, but I enjoyed it as much as she. The ball was delightful, and Emily looked her best."

"Yes, she did appear to advantage, as did you. I was very proud of you both."

"But you must not overdo. Too many nights as late as last evening could not be good for you."

"No, of course not, child. My sister-in-law will take my place occasionally. You have not met her as of yet, have you? They were late arriving for the Season. Perhaps we should pay them a call this afternoon."

As Becca agreed to her plans, Lord Roth strode into the room.

"Good morning, Lucas," Lady Roth exclaimed, a broad smile on her face. "Becca, please ring for Murdoch."

"Do not rise. I shall do it," Lord Roth said even as Becca moved to do Lady Roth's bidding. "I did not expect to see you up and about so early, Mama. Are you sure it is wise?"

"Becca has already warned me about overexerting myself. How could I possibly do so with the two of you hovering over me?"

Lord Roth avoided looking at Becca directly. She was far too fetching this morning.

"Still, you must have a care," he said. He filled his plate himself while he waited for Murdoch to appear with a new pot of tea. As he sat down, the butler rushed in, a harried look on his face.

"I am sorry, my lord."

"Is there aught amiss, Murdoch?"

"Oh, no, my lord, just a steady stream of tributes for our young ladies." The butler beamed with pride.

"Ah. It appears you were a success last evening,

Becca,'' Lucas said as Murdoch hurried to the kitchen.

Becca avoided Lord Roth's gaze and picked up her teacup. If she was receiving more attention this morning, it was because of the dowry, not her own charms, she thought.

"It seems our plan is working," Lady Roth said with a broad smile. "I did not think word would be spread so quickly."

"I told Whitechurch and Deveril yesterday at the club and they promised to inform those who asked. Also, I mentioned the family connection."

"Yes, of course." Lady Roth turned to Becca. "My dear, you have said nothing. Surely you do not mind being such a success?"

"Of course not, Aunt."

"Good. I believe I shall return to my bed, which should please you two fusspots. Becca, if you fetch today's mail to me, we shall look over the invitations."

"Of course, but—"

Realizing that Becca intended to inform Lady Roth of his request for an interview with her this morning, Lucas hurriedly intervened.

"Becca thinks, as do I, that you should rest for an hour before reading your mail."

Becca lowered her eyes. What could Lord Roth have to discuss with her that he must keep secret from his mother? It could not be Lady Roth's health, since she appeared quite robust this morning.

"You are a tyrant, darling, but I suppose I can accommodate you. Ring for Jem."

"I shall carry you, Mama. It will be the work of only a minute or two," he added, giving Becca a significant glance that told her he expected her to await his return.

"Thank you, dear," Lady Roth replied, accepting her son's offer. "Becca, stay and finish your cup of tea," she added as Becca stood. "You, too, should relax today."

"Yes. After I return Mother to her chamber, I shall keep you company." Without another word, Lord Roth swung his mother into his arms and strode from the room. Lady Roth smiled at Becca over his broad shoulder, seemingly well pleased with the turn of events.

Before Lord Roth returned from abovestairs, Lady Emily entered the breakfast room. Becca wondered if her talk with Lord Roth must be kept secret from his sister also. This interview was becoming more and more worrisome with every moment.

When Lord Roth returned to find Emily chatting away, his irritated expression told Becca not to mention their meeting to Emily, either. Therefore, she sat quietly, waiting for him to give her guidance.

Finally, after almost half an hour, he ruthlessly cut into Emily's chatter. "Sister, if you do not mind, I wish to discuss Mama's routine with Becca. I will take her off to the library so we shall not disturb your breakfast."

Lady Emily looked at her brother in surprise. "It will not disturb me, and since it concerns Mama, I should accompany you."

"There is naught to concern you," her brother assured her. "I merely wish to ensure that Mama receives enough rest and the proper nourishment."

"Actually, Emily," Becca said, anxious to conclude the private interview with Lord Roth as soon as possible, "we have a fitting at two with Madame Printemps. And then I thought we might drive through the Park."

"At two? But it is almost one o'clock now. I cannot possibly be ready!" Without another thought for her mother, Lady Emily jumped up and ran from the room.

"My thanks, Becca," Lord Roth said with an amused smile. "You clearly understand a female's thinking better than I. All the more reason for our talk. Shall we repair to the library?"

Once seated before his big desk, she watched him as she waited for him to speak.

Rather than sitting down, Lord Roth prowled the large room, his fingers occasionally reaching out to stroke the leather binding of a book. Clearing his throat, he finally said, "I must ask you not to reveal the subject of our conversation to anyone, Becca."

Becca's eyes widened as alarm coursed through her. What was he about to tell her? When he said nothing further, she realized he was waiting for her response. "Of course, Lucas."

"In the circumstances, it is, er, not easy to discuss...that is, I wish to speak of my sister."

Confusion hampered Becca's comprehension. Not having expected Emily to be the subject of their talk, she stared at him blankly.

"As her chaperon, I thought you would not object. I did not want to bother my mother." He watched her, his brow furrowed.

"No!" she exclaimed. "Of course I do not object." She gathered her thoughts and continued with more composure, "What is your concern?"

"I wondered if you had noticed my sister showing a preference for any of her suitors?" He walked over to sit on the edge of the desk, looking down at her.

"The Season has just begun. Surely it is too early—"

"Love can strike at a moment's notice, Becca. Haven't you found it so?"

She felt heat rising in her cheeks and her gaze returned to her clenched fingers. Thoughts of her first sight of the man across from her filled her mind. "I suppose so, Lucas."

"Have you noticed my sister showing a preference for any gentleman?"

His piercing stare made it difficult to dissemble, but she did not feel comfortable betraying Emily's trust. "Lucas, I—"

"Perhaps we would understand each other better, Becca, if I told you the reason for my question."

She nodded hesitantly.

He stood and paced the floor again. "Sir Anthony is my closest friend." He paused and Becca nodded again encouragingly. His words eased her mind.

"Much to my surprise, he told me after our return last evening that he is *épris* with my sister."

The surprise audible in his voice brought a smile to Becca's lips. "Your sister is quite beautiful, Lucas."

"She is attractive enough, I suppose," he responded absent-mindedly. "She certainly has a great many admirers. In any event, Sir Anthony is not yet ready to offer for her because he wants to be sure she has a regard for *him* as well as for his rank and fortune."

Well able to sympathize with Sir Anthony's feelings, Becca said, "Your sister has talked of Sir Anthony, Lucas. Last evening, of course, she was unhappy with him, but I believe that only indicates her interest."

Lord Roth frowned. "Irritation is an indication of romantic feelings?"

"Sir Anthony's comments would not have disturbed Emily were she not anxious for his regard."

An admiring look from Lord Roth flooded her with warmth and she could not help returning his smile.

"You are very wise, Becca, for one so young. Perhaps you are better suited to your position than I first thought."

"Thank you." She looked away. She found him much too overwhelming at such close quarters.

He cleared his throat and abruptly moved to the other side of his desk. "My mother and I want Emily to be happy. We would never force her to marry against her will." He paused and his gaze rested on her. She noted an arrested look, as if something had just occurred to him, but she had no idea what it could be.

"You *do* agree, don't you?"

"Of a certainty," Becca said, surprised at his question, though, of course, his enlightened attitude was not widespread among the ton. Emily was fortunate in her family.

"Your own marriage was by your choice?"

Becca's eyes widened in even greater surprise. She had almost forgotten she was supposed to be a widow. She hastily dropped her gaze, afraid he might discover her duplicity in her eyes. "Yes." There was a long silence, as if he were waiting for her to say something else, but she remained silent.

Again he cleared his throat. "Well, I would appreciate your encouraging my sister to...to entertain Tony's regard." When she did not immediately respond, he added, "He is a good man, Becca. And he cares for Emily."

"I agree, Lucas, but if the choice is to be Emily's, I do not know how much influence I may have."

"Just do your best, my dear," he replied, smiling at her once again.

Sensing that their interview was at an end, she nodded as she stood. "Very well."

When she turned to go, he added, "There is one other thing, Becca."

She paused. "Yes?"

His pleasant smile disappeared, replaced by a stern look. "Do not accept any more invitations to dance from Mr. Chancelor."

He had surprised her again. "I only danced with the gentleman once, and I could scarcely refuse his invitation if I accepted others."

"Then I shall ensure that your dance card is filled with the names of my friends each evening."

"Lucas, I am not a child," she protested.

"You are a lady and will be treated as such or the gentleman will answer to me." He had never looked more powerful or forbidding.

"Mr. Chancelor did not…that is, I did not care for his conversation, but he truly did not overstep the bounds of—"

"Do not defend him, Becca," he snapped. "I have already warned him away. His reputation precedes him."

Becca gave up the fight. With a nod of her head, she turned towards the door.

"You will inform me if he or any other gentleman does not accord you the proper respect."

Becca considered several responses but chose the one least irritating as she took the measure of the imperious man staring down at her. "Very well."

As she pulled the door closed behind her, however,

she vowed to keep her own counsel. After all, she was the chaperon, not the debutante!

BECCA RUSHED through her toilette and hurried downstairs. She discovered Emily sorting the numerous bouquets that had been delivered that morning. As Becca watched, Emily snatched the accompanying note from one of the largest and ripped it open.

A beatific smile broke across the younger girl's face and she raised the card to her lips.

"Is there anything of interest?" Becca asked, walking into the morning parlour.

Emily jumped in surprise, her cheeks flooding with colour. "No! That is, Sir Anthony sent me a note of apology. Along with a beautiful bouquet. Is that not charming?"

"Yes, quite charming." Becca suspected it would not take much effort on her part to encourage this particular romance. "You seem to have many admirers," she teased.

"Oh, several of them are for you, Becca. Are you not pleased?"

Though, in truth, she resented the bouquets a dowry had produced, she only smiled. "Of course. I shall look at the messages later, Murdoch," she said to the butler as he approached. "And please inform Lady Roth that I shall wait upon her as soon as I return."

An hour later, when the two young ladies emerged from the dressmaker's, well pleased with their selections, they discovered two gentlemen waiting in their carriage.

Lord Roth and Sir Anthony descended from the vehicle and tipped their beaver hats.

"Good afternoon, Emily, Becca. Tony and I were passing by and thought perhaps you would not object to our joining you."

"Of course not, Lucas, but Becca promised we would drive through the Park. Are you in a great hurry to return home?" Though Emily was speaking to her brother, her gaze never left Sir Anthony, which explained why she did not see the wink her brother gave Becca.

"Do you object to a ride in the Park, Tony?" Lord Roth asked, as if their plans were a surprise to him.

Becca watched his play-acting with amusement. Clearly Lucas intended to aid his friend in his courtship.

Sir Anthony quickly agreed and moved to assist Becca and Lady Emily into the carriage as Lord Roth instructed the ladies' driver to take their own carriage home.

Before she could enter the vehicle, Lord Roth leaned towards Becca and whispered, "Sit across from Emily so Tony can sit beside her."

Becca did not mind sitting with her back to the horses in aid of romance. It occurred to her that this way she would also be able to enjoy Lord Roth's company. A guilty pleasure stole through her and she avoided his eyes, afraid she might reveal her feelings.

"How fortuitous that we happened along this afternoon, isn't it, Becca?" Lord Roth murmured, a twinkle in his eye.

"I agree, my lord. Shall I keep you informed of our plans in future, so such fortunate circumstances may again occur?" she asked in a low voice.

After a quick glance to be sure the couple across from them was otherwise engaged, Lord Roth nodded. "That is an excellent plan. We shall work as a team, you and I, to be sure Emily's heart does not escape."

The warmth of his smile warned Becca that her own heart might be in as much jeopardy as Emily's. Desperate for a distraction, she turned to stare at the large collection of vehicles entering the Park.

When an unusual carriage pulled alongside theirs, she said, "Look, my lord, a pink carriage. Who is the lady? I do not recognize her."

CHAPTER SEVEN

LORD ROTH STARED at her, making Becca wonder if she had said something wrong. Lady Emily, having heard her question, leaned forward to see beyond Sir Anthony, who, after a quick glance, was looking straight ahead.

"The lady is not an acquaintance," Lord Roth said. "Tell us of your shopping expedition, Emily. Did you spend all of your allowance in one salon?" he teased, gesturing towards the packages on the floor.

"Of course not," Emily protested, distracted from the pink carriage. "We only made a few purchases."

Becca, however, had noted Lord Roth's abrupt change of subject. She had no idea what *faux pas* she had committed, but she felt sure Lord Roth would inform her at some later date. To assist in distracting Emily, she added, "We discovered sandals to match Lady Emily's pink gown for this evening."

Lady Emily batted her eyelashes at Sir Anthony. "Will you be attending the musicale this evening, sir?"

"Most assuredly. And will you perform for us, Lady Emily?" that gentleman asked gallantly.

Emily ducked her chin. "No, sir. You see, I am

not very talented musically.'' She peeped from beneath downcast lashes to determine if Sir Anthony were disappointed by her failure.

"I do not have an ear for music myself, my lady," Tony confessed with a smile. "Perhaps we may depend upon conversation for our entertainment."

"The last time we attended a musicale, we were almost thrown out because Tony insisted upon talking during the performance," Lord Roth said, a smile on his face.

Becca relaxed, since the incident at the Park entrance seemed to have been forgotten, and listened to the banter as the two gentlemen entertained Emily.

When they arrived at Roth House, however, Becca discovered Lord Roth had not forgotten.

"Emily, why don't you see if Mama wants to join you in the parlour for a visit with Sir Anthony? There is something I must discuss with Becca."

Lady Emily, with Sir Anthony occupying her mind, danced off to do her brother's bidding. Murdoch held open the parlour door for Tony and nodded in response to Lord Roth's request that tea be brought for everyone.

"May we repair to the library, please, Becca?" the master of the house asked after the door had been closed behind their guest.

"Yes, Lucas," Becca agreed. It seemed she'd spent most of the day closeted in the library with him.

Once inside, he again paced the library floor. Finally, as she watched him with a wide-eyed gaze, he said, "Becca, the, er, lady you pointed out is impure."

Becca looked at him in confusion, not sure exactly what his words meant.

In exasperation, he explained, "She is a *demimondaine.*"

Becca gasped. That word she recognized. "But—but several gentlemen were talking to her in front of everyone. And why was she there?"

"The Park is a public place, my dear. We cannot very well bar someone from visiting it because, well, because we do not approve of her."

"And I suppose I should have ignored her existence. Would that have been proper behaviour for me?"

"Of course. That is how ladies treat such occasions. That is why I felt it prudent to inform you of her identity, so in future you would not notice her."

"And the gentlemen?" Becca asked, and watched as his colour rose and he fingered his cravat as if it were too tight.

"Gentlemen have different standards of behaviour, Becca. It is the way of the world." He cleared his throat. "I am surprised you did not deduce her, er, occupation from her appearance." There was a curiosity in his voice that warned Becca to tread carefully lest she give herself away.

"There were women of ill repute in northern England, Lucas, but none so elegant, nor clearly so well established.'' The coolness of her tone did as much to convince him as her words.

''Very well. In future, try to avoid any encounters with such persons. Should it be unavoidable, just pretend the woman is not there.''

While Becca knew his directions were appropriate, given her role as his sister's chaperon, she thought it sad to treat another human in such a fashion. However, she did not voice such a radical thought to his lordship. ''Very well, Lucas.''

''Good. Shall we join the others now? I am ready for my tea.''

LORD ROTH THOUGHT, having cleared up the unfortunate incident which occurred on their outing, that tea would be a relaxing affair, with only his family, Becca and Sir Anthony present. He discovered, however, that the women in his household were quite popular. When he and Becca entered the parlour, there were several additions to their party.

Mr. Ambrose was seated beside Lady Roth, entertaining her with tidbits of gossip. Her son was struck by the teasing glances she cast at the man.

Before he could even consider intervening in that private conversation, he realized Sir Anthony was sitting alone, with a morose expression on his face, while Lady Emily entertained the three young bucks who were gathered round her. Exasperated by the turn of events, he directed a speaking look at Becca.

Her quick-wittedness was evidenced by her smooth

reorganization of the party. "Good day, gentlemen," she said. "Lady Emily, is there any more tea, or shall I ring for Murdoch?"

"There is plenty," she replied, leaning forward to pour.

"Wonderful. Lord Reeves, I would love to hear about your new carriage. And Mr. Carson, I believe you recently purchased a new pair. Have the two of you tried out your rigs against each other?"

At the prospect of a discussion of topics so dear to their hearts, the two young men abandoned Lady Emily and joined Becca across the room. Lord Roth nodded to Tony, encouraging him to take the now-vacant place next to Lady Emily, who was left with only one admirer beside her.

Once that move had been accomplished, he felt free to chaperon his mother. He greeted Mr. Ambrose and turned the conversation to their estates, which were adjacent to each other. The sparkle gradually died in his mother's eye and she turned to Becca's group for entertainment.

After a long-winded discourse on farming by Lord Roth that bored even himself, still Mr. Ambrose did not take his leave.

Lord Roth was beginning to wonder if he would run out of agricultural anecdotes when the man cleared his throat and said, "My lord, I wondered if I might be allowed to escort your mother to Mrs. O'Meara's card party tomorrow evening." Mr. Ambrose nervously waited for a response.

Lord Roth's face froze as he stared at the older man. *Damn.* He had hoped to avoid hurting his feelings. "Sir, it is kind of you to offer, but I am perfectly willing to escort my mother. It will be easier that way, you see, because of her—her infirmity."

Though Lady Roth had joined in the other conversation, she still sat near the two men and turned to look at her son. "How kind of you, Lucas. I had no idea you preferred an evening of cards to visiting with your friends." She smiled at the disappointed man sitting next to him. "We would be delighted to have you accompany us, sir, even if Lucas escorts me."

Lord Roth opened his mouth to protest, but closed it again in the face of his mother's obvious stare. "Er, yes, of course, we would be delighted if you would accompany us."

"Very well." Mr. Ambrose was beaming. "I'll come round and join you here." At Lord Roth's nod, he stood, adding, "Must be off now. Thanks for your hospitality, and I'll see you tomorrow, my dear."

Frowning at the endearment, Lord Roth rose also and shook hands, but said nothing. Lady Roth, however, smiled warmly at the gentleman and assured him she looked forward to the morrow.

As if Mr. Ambrose's departure were a signal, the other gentlemen stood also, and soon only the Roths and Becca were left in the parlour.

"Mama, do you think it wise to encourage Ambrose to hang about?" Lord Roth asked.

Raising her eyebrows, the lady said, "I enjoy his

company. I find I have a great deal in common with him.''

"But he's nothing like Papa.''

"I have not said I intend to marry Mr. Ambrose, Lucas. But I enjoy his company.''

"I think Mama ought to marry again if she wishes,'' Lady Emily chimed in, throwing a challenging look at her brother.

"There is no reason for her to remarry…unless she wishes to, of course,'' he hurriedly added. "I merely thought—''

"But I think she may be lonely. Papa's been dead for two years. Are you lonely, Mama?''

Lady Roth smiled at her children. "Darlings, I have been lonely occasionally, but I am fortunate to have you. That does not mean I must eschew the world, however.''

Lord Roth still watched his mother, a confused expression on his face. Lady Emily turned to her friend and chaperon. "You think Mama should marry again, don't you, Becca?''

Becca looked at their three faces and chose a diplomatic answer. "I think Aunt Catherine should be happy, and I believe she knows best what will make her so.''

"At my age, I ought to,'' Lady Roth said with a laugh. "And you, Becca. Will remarrying make you happy?''

Lord Roth and his sister both leaned forward, waiting for her response with great interest. Becca sought a noncommittal answer. "Time will tell."

Lady Emily was not pleased with her evasive tactics. "What does that mean, Becca? You will marry again, won't you?"

"It would certainly be wise to secure your future," Lord Roth couldn't resist adding.

"I appreciate your concern for my future, but I shall manage." In an attempt to change the subject, she asked, "Did I hear you say you intend to accompany your mother tomorrow evening to her card party?"

"Yes. What plans do you and Emily have?"

"I believe the Alexander ball is tomorrow night. Aunt Catherine intended to introduce me to her sister-in-law and niece so that we might accompany them."

"Yes, my dear, I did. Why don't we go now?" Lady Roth asked. "Cynthia will not mind receiving us this late. She is not in the least starchy."

"If you feel up to it, Aunt. Shall I tell Murdoch to summon the carriage?" Becca would have gone anywhere to avoid the line of questioning taken by the Roth siblings.

"Yes, dear, and have my maid bring down a wrap and my blue bonnet."

Becca hurried from the room.

"Emily, dear, you should not have pressed Becca about her intentions," Lady Roth said as soon as the door was closed.

"I don't see why not. I was only trying to—"

"Becca is a grown woman and free to make her own decisions," Lady Roth said gently. She smiled at her daughter's pout. "Now, are you going to accompany us to your aunt's?"

"I suppose so," Lady Emily replied, rising. "I'll go and fetch my bonnet."

Left alone with her son, Lady Roth said, "And you, my dear, must not worry so about your mother. I shall not embarrass you."

Lord Roth smiled tenderly at her. "Of course you will not. However, it is my duty to protect you."

"As you have always done," she assured him. "But I did not expect the Season to demand quite so much of you. I thought you intended to play least in sight."

"I did, Mama, though I did not realize just how many debutantes I would be launching this Season," he said, giving his mother a somewhat bewildered smile.

IT DID NOT TAKE Becca long to understand why Lady Roth would hesitate to entrust Emily's chaperonage to her sister-in-law, Lady Wixton. The lady was as hen-witted as she was charming.

She welcomed her late-arriving visitors warmly, including Becca in that warmth. Her daughter, only a few months older than Emily, was as pretty as her mother but no more generously endowed in the wits department.

"Emily!" Lady Mildred shrieked, "I have longed

to see you. Tell me how the Season is progressing. I was so vexed that we did not arrive earlier, but Tommy came down with some disgusting ailment and Mama refused to leave him.''

Emily greeted Lady Mildred and allowed herself to be drawn off to one corner to discuss recent events, though Becca doubted that Emily would be given the opportunity to speak.

Lady Wixton, like her daughter, plowed into conversation as soon as they were seated.

"Catherine, it is such a pleasure to see you up and about. I feared you would withdraw from Society. Of course, with such a pretty one to launch—'' she cast a significant look at Lady Emily ''—you will not have to expend much effort. My Mildred should go quickly, too.''

As her hostess paused to draw breath, Lady Roth managed to say, "I wondered if you would take up Emily and Becca for the Alexander ball?''

"I would be delighted to do so. It should be quite a crush. Do you remember...'' The lady then proceeded to reminisce without pause for the remainder of their visit.

Even Lady Roth, with her social skills, could not disrupt Lady Cynthia's monologue.

The butler served tea in the midst of their visit and it might have grown cold without being served had not Lady Roth motioned for Becca to do the honours. Cynthia accepted the cup as if she were a guest herself and continued to talk even as she munched on macaroons.

Becca watched in awe, never having met anyone like Lady Wixton before. When Lady Roth motioned for her to summon Jem, she slipped from the room in relief. When she returned, Lady Roth ruthlessly cut into the conversation.

"My dear Cynthia, we must depart now. Thank you for your hospitality, and Becca and Emily will await you tomorrow evening."

"Tomorrow evening?" the lady asked, surprised.

"You promised to take them with you to the Alexander ball. Do you not remember?"

"Oh, yes, of course, glad to take them anywhere. Good-looking girls," she commented absent-mindedly, as if neither were present. "My Mildred can hold her own, of course. Just as pretty as her mama," she said, patting her coiffure.

As Lady Wixton prepared to launch into another series of anecdotes, Lady Roth motioned for Jem to rescue her. He scooped her into his strong arms and marched towards the door.

"Oh, must you leave already? Well, I hope we shall see you soon," Lady Cynthia sang out.

"But—" Becca began before she was waved to silence by Lady Roth. Would they wait for Lady Wixton tomorrow evening without any hope of that lady's remembering?

When they reached the hallway, followed by Emily, who had likewise escaped her cousin's conversation, Lady Roth stopped to tell the butler to please instruct the coachman to pick up Mrs. Dunn and Lady Emily tomorrow evening on their way to the Alexander ball.

Once settled in the carriage, Becca asked, "Do you think he will remember?"

"Oh, yes. It is the only way Cynthia ever gets where she is supposed to be. He has been attending to her for years."

Becca sat quietly, as did the others, for several minutes, enjoying the blessed silence. Then she asked, "Aunt, forgive me, but is Lady Wixton your husband's sister?" Somehow, she could not picture any relationship between the woman and the Roth family.

"Heavens, no, my dear. If it were so, our intellects would be suspect. Forgive me, that was unkind. Cynthia has a good heart. No, she was the wife of my husband's younger brother. A beauty, just like Mildred, with a handsome dowry. Buckwald fell for her at first glance."

"But her name...would she not be—?"

"She married again. Buckwald died so young, only a year after their wedding. She remarried shortly thereafter, to another peer, Lord Wixton."

It amused Becca that a woman so totally oblivious to the world around her could marry well not only once, but twice. Perhaps it was the handsome dowry that drew offers. If her own dowry were known—not the one the Roths had provided, but that given by her father—Becca knew she, too, would have her choice of the ton. Even Lord Roth would…no, she mustn't even consider such a thing. She did not want to buy a husband.

Not that Lord Roth had need of her funds, but he had admitted he would not refuse a dowry, and she also owned numerous properties that conferred power as well as wealth.

She chewed her lower lip in despair. She could not marry where her heart led her, because she was living a lie. She *would* not marry if the object of her affection only wanted her because of her true dowry. Any man who chose her for that reason alone could never give her the kind of marriage she sought. Her heart ached as she dispelled the picture of Lord Roth her mind summoned.

"Are you uncomfortable, my dear?"

Jolted from her thoughts by Lady Roth, Becca summoned a smile. "Of course not, Aunt. I was thinking of which gown I should wear this evening. Do you accompany us to the musicale?"

"Yes, I believe I shall. I feel quite well, and I do enjoy music."

"Sir Anthony will be there." Lady Emily added, "He does not mind that I am not musically gifted."

The other ladies smiled at her pink cheeks.

"I'm sure he does not, my dear," her mother said. "He seems most appreciative of your other attributes. Will your brother escort us?"

Lady Emily looked questioningly at Becca, and she

shrugged her shoulders. "I do not believe Lucas indicated his intentions."

"What did he discuss with you in the library, then?" Lady Emily asked, remembering their disappearance when they arrived home from the Park.

Becca's own cheeks reddened as she confessed, "He wished to explain my mistake." With a sideways glance at Lady Roth, she said, "I accidently made reference to a person who is a member of the *demimonde*."

Though Lady Roth's eyebrows lifted, she made no comment. Lady Emily, however, exclaimed, "Was that the lady in the pink carriage?"

Becca nodded.

"Well, why didn't Lucas say so? He simply ignored Becca's question."

"I suppose your brother was embarrassed. Men do not readily discuss such things before their sisters."

"Does my brother have a—a mistress?" Lady Emily demanded, leaning forward with interest. She was not the only one curious.

"I do not know. I would never question him on such a subject." Lady Roth stared straight ahead, looking at neither young lady. "Young men sometimes, before marriage, indulge in such liaisons."

"I've heard they do so even after marriage," Lady Emily muttered.

"Child, I do not know where you get these notions. You must never make such statements in public. Or to your brother."

"I will not, Mama," Emily said. "But I will not allow *my* husband to abuse me so. He will be true to me or he will regret it."

Becca thought Emily's attitude a perfectly reasonable one.

CHAPTER EIGHT

LORD ROTH DID accompany them to the musicale. And though his sister cast several strange looks his way, she did not ask the question that had burned on her lips since their return from Lady Wixton's.

Becca, too, would have liked to ask that same question. Not that she had any interest in Lord Roth, she assured herself, since any alliance in that quarter would be impossible. Or in any quarter, for that matter.

Numerous young men flocked round the two ladies that evening, entertaining them between musical numbers and keeping them company while they listened to various performers. Sir Anthony was among those surrounding Lady Emily.

"Such caterwauling should not be allowed in public," he murmured in her ear as a young lady attempted to demonstrate her proficiency. Lady Emily giggled and received several condemning looks from some members of the performer's family who were nearby.

Becca breathed a sigh of relief when the young woman ended her performance. She was sympathetic to Lady Emily's response but felt she ought to be

careful not to insult others. An intermission was
called and she promptly stood. Lord Roth, who had
not taken a seat with them, appeared in front of her.
"Shall we find some refreshment to remove the taste
of the last performance?"

"*Shh*, my lord," she whispered. "Do not offend
her family. They are seated very near."

He took her elbow and nodded to Tony to follow.
Easing their way through the crowd, he found a table
in a corner of the dining parlour and pulled out a chair
for Becca. "If you will wait here, my dear, I'll fetch
something to tempt your appetite."

Lady Emily joined Becca, and the two gentlemen
strolled away. "The performances have been intoler-
able," she whispered to her chaperon.

"I will admit a respite is welcome." She absent-
mindedly watched the crowd move in front of them.

"Well!" Emily exclaimed, sitting straighter.

"What is it?"

"Sir Anthony is conversing with Miss Greenwood
instead of bringing me some punch."

Becca saw the gentleman bend to hear some comment from the lips of a charming young woman who
was fluttering her lashes at a furious rate.

"I'm sure he has only stopped for a moment. Probably the young lady asked a question of him. After
all, Sir Anthony is quite sought-after."

Lady Emily was not appeased by Becca's words.
She glared at the twosome until Sir Anthony moved

on towards the serving tables and a disappointed Miss Greenwood seated herself in a nearby chair.

When the two gentlemen returned with a wide assortment of delicacies, Sir Anthony did not receive a warm welcome.

"Lady Emily, is something amiss? Have I failed to provide you with what you would wish?" he asked, confused by her change in attitude.

"Not at all, Sir Anthony. I am just surprised that you found your way back to our table at all."

Both men seemed struck by her petulant response, and Becca attempted to rescue the evening. "I believe Lady Emily feared Miss Greenwood might demand your presence, Sir Anthony."

"I did not fear it! If he prefers her company to mine, that is his choice."

Concern marring his brow, Sir Anthony hastened to reassure her. "My dear Lady Emily, I prefer no one's company to yours. The lady only stopped me to ask my opinion of her performance." With a smile designed to coax the young lady from her sullens, he added, "I'm afraid I was less than candid. Had I told the truth, she might have slapped my face in front of everyone."

Lady Emily's sense of the ridiculous responded to his teasing and she smiled. "I am grateful you did not cause such a scene."

When he offered the lobster patties this time, she willingly accepted them and an awkward moment was averted. Becca breathed a sigh of relief and looked up to discover Lord Roth watching her, a matching smile on his face.

"And have *you* enjoyed the music this evening?" Lord Roth asked.

"The performances have been most interesting, my lord," Becca replied.

"A tactful response, Becca. Are you sure you do not wish to enter the lists? I believe our hostess would be pleased to allow you the stage."

"I am not a debutante."

"But you are seeking a husband, are you not?" he asked, his gaze remaining on her.

"No, my lord," she assured him firmly, wondering why he persisted in this line of questioning.

"But my mother—"

"I believe we are being summoned to our chairs for more entertainment. Shall we go?"

She stood and he, perforce, rose with her. Before he could pursue his questioning, she asked, "Did you ensure that Lady Roth was served?"

"I would have, but Mr. Ambrose remains at her side, willing to meet her every need. My presence seemed superfluous."

She noted his concerned air. To soothe him, she suggested, "Perhaps you should ask your mother if she is too tired to remain. I would not object to an early night."

"Brilliant, my dear. Any escape from the entertainment provided this evening would be acceptable in my book." He turned to inform Tony and Emily of his intention, indicating he hoped to persuade his mother to claim exhaustion due to her infirmity, and all four strolled over to Lady Roth's chair.

Lady Roth was willing to accommodate her family, and even Mr. Ambrose, invited to accompany them back to Roth House for a cup of tea, did not object and accepted the offer to ride in Sir Anthony's curricle. After a few words with their hostess, Lucas joined the others in the Roth carriage.

"That is the last musicale I shall attend for a long time," he exclaimed as he sank back against the squabs.

"It was miserable this evening, was it not?" Lady Roth asked. "All the same, I feel guilty using my infirmity as an excuse to escape. But poor George did not think he could bear much more."

"George?" Lord Roth demanded sharply.

"Mr. Ambrose, of course. His name is George, dear."

"I know his name, Mama. I was merely surprised that you used it."

"Really? I thought you young people were always so familiar with close friends," the lady said serenely, ignoring her son's stare.

"Perhaps Mr. Ambrose would enjoy a hand of cards with you and the two gentlemen when we return home, Aunt," Becca suggested, hoping to change the direction of the conversation. She knew Lord Roth would not care for the idea, but it would please Lady Roth.

"What a delightful proposal, my dear," Lady Roth responded. "You do not mind, do you, Lucas? It would help George and me to sharpen our skills for the card party tomorrow. It has been several years since I have played."

His mother's pleasure made it impossible for Lord Roth to refuse, but he shot a frown at Becca. She felt sure she would receive his displeasure later.

Since Mr. Ambrose was riding in Sir Anthony's vehicle, following the Roth carriage, he did not learn of the treat in store for him until their arrival at Roth House. He was almost as pleased as Lady Roth. Sir Anthony, on the other hand, having hoped for an intimate conversation with his beloved, reluctantly agreed to be the fourth.

The two gentlemen posed no challenge to the wits of the older couple. Lady Emily, unhappy to be ignored, paraded about the room at various intervals, drawing Sir Anthony's eye at the most critical moments and causing him to misplay his cards.

Becca, sitting quietly on the sofa doing needlework she'd fetched from her room, did nothing to distract the players. Lord Roth's gaze, however, frequently flew to her as he waited for his turn to play. The fact that he had to be called to attention numerous times did not alter his behaviour.

Lady Roth, watching her cards as well as the deportment of those at the table, had a smile on her face. Yes, things were going well, she thought as she laid down the winning hand.

LORD ROTH SAT in the library, estate papers before him, but his gaze fixed on nothing in particular. The events of the previous evening occupied his mind. So Becca claimed she was not seeking a husband. His growing fascination with the lovely widow made him hope she might not change her mind until after the Season was ended.

While marriage was not something he had so far seriously contemplated, it seemed more and more attractive the longer he knew Becca. But as long as she resided under his roof, of course, he could not pursue his interest.

A knock on the door followed by Murdoch's entrance interrupted his thoughts.

"My lord, a Mr. Tyndall is here to see you."

Frowning, Lord Roth stood. "Show him in, Murdoch." Why would Tyndall call upon him? The man was several years his senior and ran with a different crowd, one much more attuned to gambling dens and mistresses.

"Good morning, my lord. Thank you for receiving me," the man said as he strode into the library.

Lord Roth gestured to a chair and circled the desk to sit behind it. The blue superfine jacket and yellow waistcoat his guest wore was elegant dress for a chance-met visit.

"I suppose you know why I am here," Mr. Tyndall said, a smile on his face.

"Frankly, I can't fathom a reason, sir, but I feel sure you will inform me."

Mr. Tyndall's eyebrows rose. "Then I must be the first to approach you. I am relieved. I was afraid I might be left at the post." With a satisfied smirk, he settled into his chair.

"You still have me at a loss, sir." Lucas could not keep a certain coldness from his voice. If the man had come to ask for his sister's hand, as he now supposed, he would indeed find himself left at the post.

"I have come to ask for Mrs. Dunn's hand in marriage."

Lord Roth grew still as he heard Tyndall's words. Finally, he said, "Do you have any reason to suppose that Mrs. Dunn looks favourably upon your suit?" His fingers clenched into fists as he waited for a response.

Mr. Tyndall smiled. "Ladies do not find me unattractive, my lord, if I may say so in all due modesty." Something in his host's glare must have warned the man of his feelings. Tyndall cleared his throat, the smile disappearing, and added, "I have visited with Mrs. Dunn on several occasions and she did not show any aversion to me."

"And you consider lack of aversion to be sufficient reason for marriage?"

"Come now, my lord, surely you do not hold the view that *love* should be an ingredient." The man laughed, but he was growing more and more uncomfortable. "Besides, while the lady is a charmer, her portion is not so large as to attract a title."

Lord Roth wanted to show the man the door, but

he had no idea whether Becca would consider his offer. He stood and reached for the bell-pull. "Perhaps we should inform Mrs. Dunn of your intentions."

"Is that necessary? After all, it is a business arrangement. Can we not settle the matter between us?"

"No, Mr. Tyndall, we cannot. Mrs. Dunn is of age and has the right to accept or decline your offer according to her wishes." Murdoch opened the door and Lord Roth asked that Mrs. Dunn be summoned. After the butler's departure, the two men sat in silence, awaiting the widow's arrival.

BECCA WAS IN HER ROOM, enjoying a cup of tea. She'd avoided the breakfast parlour that morning, certain Lord Roth would vent his spleen over being forced to play cards last evening. If she avoided him this morning, perhaps he would feel less strongly about it. Though, of course, she knew he would not be too severe, since his mother had been pleased.

When Murdoch informed her that his lordship wished to see her in the library, she sighed. Obviously he was not going to let her escape so easily. She checked her appearance in the cheval glass, tucking a stray hair into place and noting with dismay the way her cheeks flooded with colour at the thought of an interview with Lord Roth.

She considered changing her gown, but set the notion aside. After all, one did not dress to receive a lecture. And she must not encourage her fantasies.

When she entered the library, she was surprised to discover Lord Roth was not alone. She greeted both men before looking at Lucas with a question in her eyes.

"Please be seated, Mrs. Dunn." Lord Roth waited until she had done so, then gestured for Mr. Tyndall to resume his seat. Lucas, however, remained standing. "Mr. Tyndall has called this morning on a special errand."

Becca offered the man a polite smile, wondering why she should be called, unless, of course, the man had arrived after his lordship had sent for her. She sat quietly, wondering if she should offer to wait in the parlour until he was free.

"I felt you should be present, since it concerns you."

Her gaze flew to Lord Roth's face, her green eyes questioning, but she said nothing.

"Mr. Tyndall has requested your hand in matrimony."

The colour fled from Becca's cheeks as she stared at Lord Roth. The man next to her stirred.

"His lordship has failed to mention how greatly I esteem you, Mrs. Dunn. I feel our marriage would bring both of us many years of happiness." His smile did not warm Becca's heart.

After another look at Lord Roth, Becca said carefully, "Thank you for the honour you do me, Mr. Tyndall, but I must refuse your kind offer."

The smile was wiped from his face. "Surely you

will at least take time to consider my offer, Mrs. Dunn. After all, in some quarters I am considered quite a catch.''

Becca refused the temptation to ask him to name those quarters, since he was well known to be a game-ster, with his pockets continuously to let. She simply said, "I'm sorry, Mr. Tyndall, but I am unable to do so.''

Her gaze left the man's reddening face, and turned to Lord Roth. His pleased smile was her reward.

"Thank you for calling, Tyndall," he said, extend-ing a hand to the man and leaving him little option but to rise and take it. "Perhaps we shall see you at some of the entertainments in the future.''

"But, my lord, as gentlemen, could we not—''

"Goodbye, Mr. Tyndall," Lord Roth said, over-riding the man's protests and escorting him to where Murdoch was waiting.

Becca did not stir from her chair. Somehow she knew Lucas would not let her depart without some conversation between them.

He strolled back into the library and took the chair Tyndall had occupied. "A wise decision, my dear," he said.

"Thank you, Lucas." When he said nothing fur-ther, she challenged him with her gaze. "Is there any-thing else?''

"A small matter of trapping me at the card table last evening," he said, but she was relieved to see a teasing smile on his lips.

"It pleased your mother."

"I know, and that is the only reason I forgive you."

She looked away from the warmth of his regard. The library seemed much smaller than its normal size, lending an intimacy to their conversation that sent tremors through her limbs. "I—I must wait upon your mother, Lucas, if there is nothing else."

"No, Becca, there is nothing more." As she reached the door, however, he called to her. "I meant to enquire if you ride."

Becca's thoughts flashed back to her younger years when she and her father had raced across pastures, leaping fences, exulting in the beauty of the outdoors. Her cheeks flushed with pleasure. "Yes, I ride, but I do not have a riding habit."

"Ah. Please have my mother order you one at once. I believe Emily will show to advantage on horseback in the Park, and she must be accompanied by her chaperon, of course."

Her heart leapt at the thought of riding once more. Even a sedate trot in the Park would be wonderful. "Thank you, Lucas. I would delight in accompanying Emily."

"Do you miss the countryside very much?"

Becca looked away from his sympathetic glance. "I enjoy London, but, yes, I miss the country life."

"Did the lady you worked for in…Bath, was it?…provide you with a mount?"

Having almost forgotten her fictional employer,

Becca said, "Er, no, my lord, she was an elderly lady and did not keep a stable other than for her carriage horses."

"Then your return to horseback will be all the more enjoyable. Let me know as soon as your habit is ready. I believe Emily already has one."

"Yes, I shall." She slipped from the room, a smile on her face. Her earlier avoidance of Lucas seemed silly now. Not only was he not unhappy with her, he had offered to provide her with a horse and an elegant riding habit. Perhaps she could visit the dressmaker this very morning. With a happy skip, she ran up the stairs to consult with Lady Roth.

LORD ROTH SAT behind his desk, a pensive look on his face. So far, the morning had been most enlightening. It had warmed his heart that Becca had rejected the offer of matrimony without a moment's hesitation.

Not that Mr. Tyndall was much of a catch, but many ladies would have considered him. Becca had not, even for a moment.

He must pay a visit at once to Tattersall's to find an appropriate mount for her. It should have occurred to him earlier, but he frequently found himself distracted when in the woman's presence. He pictured her in his mind's eye, mounted on a well-behaved filly, racing in the wind, her dark curls streaming behind her.

After the Season, could he persuade her to visit his mother and him at High Oaks? Becca would like his estate, he was sure. It was unusual to discover a woman as beautiful as Becca who could be content in the country without the fashionable shops, the parties, the theatre. But then, he was discovering her to be an unusual woman in many ways.

Not the least of which was the fact that she could not remember where she had lived for two years of her life. He suddenly remembered that Emily had told him the widow had lived in Nottingham while she was companion to an elderly lady. But he had mentioned Bath and she had accepted the change of locale without so much as a blink.

Either she was a very forgetful female, or she had lied about her past.

CHAPTER NINE

LORD ROTH SPENT a pleasant afternoon at Tattersall's in Sir Anthony's company. It was made more enjoyable because he found the perfect mare for Becca. Its coal black coat would match her thick curls, and its frisky pace would please her.

His thoughts dwelt on morning rides, he astride his stallion, Inferno, riding side by side with the lovely widow.

"Don't Lady Emily already have a mount?" Sir Anthony enquired when Lord Roth first began bidding.

"Yes. We didn't bring her mare to Town with us, but I have sent for it."

"Then why are you purchasing another lady's mount?"

"For Becca, so that she may accompany Emily on rides in the Park. Shall you join us as soon as the ladies are properly outfitted?"

"Without a doubt. I go wherever Lady Emily appears. I think she enjoys my company."

"You are too modest, my friend," Lord Roth teased. "My sister always looks for you as soon as she arrives at any entertainment."

While Sir Anthony revelled in his friend's words, Lord Roth added, "I assume, then, you will be attending the Alexander ball this evening?"

"Yes. I have already engaged Lady Emily for two dances, one of them the supper dance," Sir Anthony added proudly.

"Ask Becca to join you for the meal, if you don't mind. My mother will not be there this evening, and Lady Wixton will probably not even remember that the pair accompanied her to the ball."

Sir Anthony looked closely at his friend. "You feel the chaperon needs a chaperon?"

"Not exactly." Lord Roth continued to examine the finer points of the horses being auctioned off. "But I don't think she is as experienced as she would have the world believe."

"Very well. I'll keep an eye on Mrs. Dunn also," his friend replied, and Lord Roth had to be satisfied with that.

He discovered, however, that his absence from the ball bothered him more than he would have considered possible. Many times that evening his thoughts were fixed on Becca and the partners who would be fortunate enough to dance with her. He wished he were there instead of making up a fourth for his mother, Mr. Ambrose and Lady Cather.

"My lord!" Lady Cather shrieked, once more drawing his attention back to the card table. "Please have the goodness not to trump my lead! What were you thinking of?"

He humbly apologized and promised to pay closer attention to the cards. When he looked up, he discovered his mother watching him, amusement in her eyes.

"You enjoy my humiliation, Mama?" he whispered.

"You are the one who insisted on coming, child," she returned. "You must suffer the consequences."

BECCA CIRCLED the ballroom in the arms of a new acquaintance, Mr. Carouthers, hoping the music would end soon. The man held her too closely as they waltzed. However, she soon discovered that his interest lay not with her, but with her charge.

"Lady Emily is quite beautiful," he said, smiling at Becca. He put her in mind of a wolf circling a lamb.

"Indeed."

"Is she attached as of yet?"

Though she wished she could respond differently, she shook her head.

"Ah. She is a graceful dancer. And charming."

Becca sighed with relief when the dance ended. She only hoped the man had not yet signed Lady Emily's dance card. She would warn her to avoid him. When he delivered her to Lady Cynthia, however, he immediately claimed Lady Emily's next dance.

Becca's next dance partner was Sir Anthony, and she offered to stroll about the room rather than dance if he would like. Having performed every dance so far, with numerous young ladies presented to him by his hostess, Sir Anthony was relieved to be given a respite.

"You are enjoying yourself, Mrs. Dunn?" he asked as he took her arm.

"Yes, Sir Anthony. Do you know the gentleman dancing with Lady Emily now?"

Without looking, he murmured, "A Mr. Carouthers, I believe. We were introduced this evening."

Becca could not think of a polite way to phrase her question. Sir Anthony prompted her. "Is there something amiss? Did he behave in a ungentlemanly manner?"

"No, sir, but—but I did not care for him. And he showed a great interest in Lady Emily."

"Ah. Thank you for warning me, my dear. I promised Lucas I would keep an eye on the two of you." His concerned gaze picked out the dancing couple, and the sight of Lady Emily's rosy cheeks and smiling lips did not please him. "She does not appear to have any objection to the gentleman."

"She is very young, Sir Anthony. I do not think I am betraying her confidence when I say that she enjoys your company above that of all others."

"Thank you. I am some ten years her senior. Because she is so young, I did not want to rush her into an engagement, but the longer I wait to declare myself, the more unnerving it is. I am afraid she will find another she prefers.'' His eyes remained fixed on the laughing young blonde, her pale peach skirt swirling around her.

"I do not believe she is too young to know her own heart." Becca felt sure Lord Roth would not oppose her hints to Sir Anthony. She, too, was afraid Lady Emily might be distracted by others from choosing the right husband. Becca agreed with Lord Roth. Sir Anthony was a good man.

He squeezed her hand. "Thank you for the encouragement, my dear. Will you join Lady Emily and myself for supper?"

"That would be delightful, sir. I am partnered with Mr. Arbuthnot."

The laughter in her eyes was not unkind, but Sir Anthony groaned. "That puppy! Ah, well, he will keep us entertained."

In fact, supper was not entertaining for Sir Anthony, but it was not Mr. Arbuthnot's fault. Mr. Carouthers, accompanied by a shy young lady, joined their table at Lady Emily's invitation.

Practically ignoring his own partner, Mr. Carouthers flattered and flirted with Lady Emily to the exclusion of all others. Sir Anthony's face grew sterner with each passing moment.

When he led Lady Emily to the dance floor after they had supped, Sir Anthony could not hide his displeasure. "I do not believe your brother would approve of your companions."

She looked up in surprise. "What do you mean?"

"Mr. Carouthers. You scarcely know the man and yet you flirted outrageously with him." He pressed his lips firmly together. He hadn't intended to criticize her.

Lady Emily, never happy to hear strictures on her behaviour, was particularly upset to have them come from Sir Anthony. "I beg your pardon! I behaved perfectly."

"And Carouthers? Do you consider his behaviour to be exemplary? Poor Miss Boliver was heartily ignored by her own escort."

The dance movements separated them. By the time they came back together, Sir Anthony had himself well in hand. Lady Emily, however, did not.

"If you are so concerned for Miss Boliver, why do you not console her? You have certainly flirted as much as Mr. Carouthers. I do not believe you sat out a single dance."

He stared at her in surprise. "Would you have me ignore the plea of my hostess to dance with some of the less-popular young ladies? I am allowed only two dances with you. The sole alternative would be to lean against the wall and stare at you like some Byronic figure."

They separated once again, but he watched her in frustration. What was she about? When he again reached her side, she froze him with her cold stare.

"It matters not to me how you comport yourself, Sir Anthony. After all, I have no hold on you." Nor did she sound as if she wanted anything to do with him in future.

The music ended and he was given no more opportunity to speak with her. The moment they reached Lady Wixton's side, Lady Emily was claimed by her next partner, and Sir Anthony was left standing helplessly by the chaperon.

"La, Sir Anthony, have you danced with my lovely Mildred yet?" Lady Wixton demanded, shoving the young debutante at him.

"Yes, I have had that pleasure, my lady, and look forward to dancing with her again in future. Now, if you will excuse me," he said hastily, backing away. For the rest of the evening, he leaned against a column and stared darkly at Lady Emily and her various partners, for all the world like some Byronic figure.

BECCA CONSIDERED discussing her concerns about Mr. Carouthers with Lady Emily upon their arrival home that evening. However, it was apparent Emily was out of sorts, as was Sir Anthony, and she decided to wait until morning.

She rose early and hurried down to breakfast. She had much to do that day; her haste was assuredly not because she hoped to see Lord Roth. After all, she had seen him yesterday morning. It was not as if the man were essential to her happiness. Her face fell when she entered the morning-room to find it empty.

Lingering through her breakfast, Becca sat in lonely splendor, with none of the Roths appearing.

When Murdoch returned with a second pot of tea, she ventured a question. "Has Lord Roth already breakfasted?"

"Yes, Mrs. Dunn. He departed early on business."

"Oh." Suddenly the day appeared flat and uninteresting.

"Chef asked if he might consult with you about the menu for Lady Emily's ball, Mrs. Dunn, when you had a free moment." Murdoch watched her worriedly. He could scarcely understand the man, much less appease him.

"Of course, Murdoch, I shall come down now."

When she left the kitchen more than an hour later, the French chef had been satisfied that he was well appreciated and that his menu for the ball was perfection. The fact that the items on it hadn't changed a whit from those Lady Roth had requested was a testament to Becca's diplomacy.

Lady Emily had descended for breakfast, then returned to her room again while Becca was occupied in the kitchen. With Lady Roth awaiting her to look through the mail, Becca once more postponed her talk with her charge. After all, they would not see Mr. Carouthers again until that evening.

She discovered her error when she left Lady Roth's chamber and rapped on Lady Emily's door. Her maid opened it and answered Becca's question as to Lady Emily's whereabouts.

"She'm gone for a ride with a Mr. Carouthers, ma'am."

Becca frowned. Since neither she nor Lady Roth had been notified that Mr. Carouthers had come to call, it appeared that the invitation had been extended the previous evening. Further questioning of the maid confirmed Becca's supposition.

Becca returned to Lady Roth's chamber. "Aunt Catherine, I am a little concerned."

"Yes, my dear, what is it? Has Emily been naughty?" Lady Roth asked with a chuckle from her bed.

"No. That is, she accepted an invitation from a gentleman to go for a ride in the Park."

Lady Roth's eyebrows rose. "That is perfectly acceptable, my dear, as long as it is not a closed carriage and his tiger accompanies them."

"I know. We met the gentleman last evening, but something about him bothers me. It is nothing I can explain, Aunt, but—but I did not care for him."

"What is his name?" Lady Roth did not question Becca's instinct.

"Mr. Timothy Carouthers. Lady Sandifer introduced him."

"Hmm. She is acceptable enough. But I have not heard of Mr. Carouthers. Did Sir Anthony know the gentleman?"

"I did ask Sir Anthony, but he met him last evening for the first time also." Becca paused before adding, "Mr. Carouthers and Miss Boliver joined us for supper. And I believe Emily and Sir Anthony grew cross with each other."

"Do not concern yourself, my dear. You have done all that is proper by bringing your concern to me. I shall have a word with Emily."

Becca intended to talk to Lady Emily also. To that purpose, she settled in the front parlour with her stitchery and waited for her charge's return.

When Lady Emily did come back, she brought Mr. Carouthers with her. "Becca, I have asked Mr. Carouthers to take tea with us. You do not object?"

"Of course not. Good day, Mr. Carouthers." Becca smiled at the man, trying to keep her feelings towards him from showing. Perhaps she'd been precipitous in her judgement.

"Good day, Mrs. Dunn. It is a lovely day, isn't it, though, of course, not as lovely as Lady Emily." He directed a longing gaze at the object of his flattery.

"Were there many people in the Park?" Becca asked, repulsed by his behaviour.

"A few," he said, though his gaze never left Lady Emily. "None as beautiful as my companion. She is the most charming lady I have ever met."

Becca stared at Emily's blushing cheeks, wondering that she could fall so completely under the spell of the man.

"Are you recently come to London, Mr. Carouthers? I do not remember seeing you at earlier entertainments."

"Yes, I arrived late for the Season. Though I would have hurried from my estates had I known such loveliness awaited me."

Becca wondered if he would turn each statement into a compliment for Lady Emily. And if so, could the young lady possibly believe every word?

"Ah, where are your estates located?" At least his opening would give her an opportunity to discover something about him.

His gaze swung to Becca and sharpened instantly. Then he looked again at Lady Emily in a lovesick fashion. "In northern England. Too far away for you to have heard of them."

"I have visited the North Country, sir. Just exactly where are your holdings?"

Again she received a sharp look. "The closest town is Pickering. I have extensive land in that neighbourhood."

Since Becca's father's estates were in that precise area and she herself now owned several large parcels of land there, she thought the man must be lying.

Just as she considered another question to interrupt the tête-à-tête he was enjoying on the sofa with Lady Emily, the door opened. Lord Roth and Sir Anthony strolled in, though Sir Anthony paused when he recognized the occupants.

"Good day, ladies," Lord Roth said, a smile on his face, but Becca noted that his eyes narrowed as he studied their guest.

"My lord," she said hurriedly, "may I present Mr. Carouthers? We made his acquaintance last evening through Lady Sandifer, and he was kind enough to take Lady Emily for a ride in the Park today."

Mr. Carouthers had risen, and he and Lord Roth shook hands. Sir Anthony acknowledged his presence coolly. Since Sir Anthony himself received no warmer greeting from Lady Emily, who presented him with a curt nod, he chose the seat beside Becca.

Awkward conversation was carried on for the next few minutes. Lady Emily refused to speak to Sir Anthony, who ignored the presence of Mr. Carouthers, who avoided Mrs. Dunn. Lord Roth watched the goings-on curiously. When Mr. Carouthers finally rose to depart, no one, not even Lady Emily, begged him to extend his stay.

He bowed over Lady Emily's hand and promised to see her that evening. His leave-taking of Becca was considerably briefer, as were his words to the gentlemen. Once the door closed behind him, Sir Anthony stated the purpose of his visit.

"Lady Emily, I wish to extend an apology for speaking as I did last evening. I had no right to instruct you on your behaviour."

If he had hoped for an immediate thawing, he was disappointed. Lady Emily stared down her nose at him and acknowledged his apology with a slight nod.

"That was a very handsome apology, Tony. What brought it about?" Lord Roth asked, eyeing his sister.

"My jealousy led me to criticize Lady Emily when I should not have." He, too, continued to look at Lady Emily. His generous admission was more warmly received than his apology.

"I forgive you, Sir Anthony," Lady Emily said

sweetly. "Indeed, Mr. Carouthers was just being friendly, as he was today."

"Much friendlier and he would be on his knees proposing," Sir Anthony could not keep from muttering.

Immediately Lady Emily stiffened again. "You insult me to even suggest such a thing. I only met the man last evening."

"I'm sure Sir Anthony did not mean to offend you, dear," Becca said quickly. "Mr. Carouthers *is* rather fulsome in his compliments."

"I saw nothing out of the ordinary. Perhaps you are miffed because he did not take notice of you."

"Emily, you will apologize to Becca for that childish remark," Lord Roth said sternly.

Before Lady Emily could protest, as it was clear she intended to do, Sir Anthony rose. "I shall excuse myself and be off. I apologize for intruding." He took Becca's hand in farewell, shook Lord Roth's, and only nodded in Lady Emily's direction before departing.

The spurned lady sniffed in outrage, her nose high in the air.

"Your apology, Sister," Lord Roth reminded her sternly.

"I do not see the need." When he stared at her unrelentingly, she added, "Oh, very well, I apologize, Becca. But Mr. Carouthers was all that was proper."

Becca said nothing, steadily plying her needle and avoiding looking at the other two. Lord Roth re-

sponded in her stead. "He may be all that is proper,
but do not accept any more invitations from him until
I am certain he is. Since he is unknown to us, I must
discover his history."

"You are being too ridiculous, Lucas! Anyone can
see that he is a gentleman. You are simply being difficult because of Sir Anthony!"

Lord Roth frowned at his sister. "Even were Tony
not involved, I would insist on knowing more about
any man who pursued my sister. But I would warn
you that I do not want to see Tony hurt. So have a
care, little sister."

"Tony? What about me? Do you not care that he
has wounded *me?*" Emily asked dramatically, rising
to stare at her brother. "I have been all that is pleasing to Sir Anthony, and he dared to question my com-
portment. The fault is with him, not with me!" She
ran to the door, where she stopped to face her brother
once more. "At least Mr. Carouthers does not carp at
me!"

Wisely not waiting for a response, Lady Emily
dashed out of the room and up the stairs.

Outraged by his sister's behaviour, Lord Roth
swung around to the only other occupant of the room.
"You will see that my sister follows my dictates in
this matter, Becca."

"I will do my best, Lucas," Becca said calmly.

"I shall leave instructions with Murdoch not to admit the fellow. That should do the trick."

"Will it not also upset Lady Emily unnecessarily?

After all, I do not believe there is any harm in Mr. Carouthers, even though I do not find him pleasing.''

"You don't?''

"No, but I shall keep a close eye on Lady Emily until you have determined the man's character.''

Becca's calm demeanour did much to soothe Lord Roth. He sat down on the sofa beside her. "Very well. Have you ordered a riding habit?''

The change of subject surprised her. "Why, yes, I did so yesterday.''

"When will it be ready?''

"Madame Printemps promised it for tomorrow.'' Becca's cheeks flushed with excitement at the thought of riding again.

"Very well, the day after, I shall introduce you to the mare you will ride. Her name is Satin and I believe you will be well pleased with her.''

"She sounds delightful, Lucas. I shall look forward to making her acquaintance.''

CHAPTER TEN

WITH THE PROSPECT of a ride to look forward to, Becca expected the next two days to drag on interminably as she anticipated her treat. However, Fate had other plans.

Because Lady Roth had accepted an invitation to join a group at the theatre, Lady Emily and Becca were once again left in the care of Lady Wixton. Lord Roth, much to his mother's and Becca's amusement, immediately offered his escort to his mother.

"It is quite unnecessary, Lucas. Mr. Ambrose is sure to agree to escort me." Lady Roth presented an innocent façade to her son, but Becca noticed the twinkle in her eye.

"I do not wish to cause Ambrose any inconvenience," he said.

"But the girls will have no escort except Cynthia."

"Aunt Cynthia is quite satisfactory as a chaperon," Lady Emily quickly asserted, reminding Becca that the young lady was unhappy with her brother. "Besides, Becca will be with me."

"That is true, child. Perhaps, for once, your brother could have his evening free to join his friends, rather than chasing after the females in his family."

Lord Roth showed no appreciation for his mother's suggestion. "I would prefer to accompany you, Mama. Especially since Tony insists on following Emily to every entertainment in any case. "

Sir Anthony, however, resisted the urge to follow Lady Emily that evening. The two young ladies were collected by Lady Wixton—Lady Roth having prudently sent a note to her sister-in-law's butler—on her way to Lady Hunsaker's ball.

Lady Emily's eyes had a feverish cast, Becca noticed as she walked beside her charge up the steps. "Are you feeling well, Emily?"

The sudden flush of her companion's cheeks did not reassure Becca. "Yes, of course. I'm feeling quite well. The evening should be most enjoyable."

"I hope you and Sir Anthony will not remain at odds," Becca added as a gentle hint. "He is an admirable man, and many young ladies would enjoy his company."

"Many young women ladies *have* enjoyed his company!" Lady Emily exclaimed, a touch of bitterness in her voice.

Becca said nothing else. It appeared Emily was not ready to forgive. After greeting their hostess and her daughter, they followed Lady Wixton into the crowded ballroom. Immediately Becca, Lady Emily and Lady Mildred were surrounded by gentlemen eager to sign their dance cards.

Becca was not so distracted that she did not notice Mr. Carouthers's eager approach to Lady Emily, nor the young lady's encouragement as he signed her card twice. It appeared Lady Emily did not intend to heed her brother's advice. Unfortunately, Becca could think of no way to convince her to do so.

Spying Lady Sandifer across the room, however, she decided a closer acquaintance with the person who'd introduced Mr. Carouthers to them would be in order.

A short time later, she'd manoeuvred her way to the other side of the ballroom and stopped next to Lady Sandifer.

"Good evening, my lady. It is such an enjoyable evening, is it not?"

The overly stout lady fanned herself vigorously as she answered. "Yes, yes. A delightful romp. A little warm, perhaps."

"Would you care to walk out on the balcony? I think it is quite cool out of doors."

"A marvellous idea, young lady. Shall you accompany me?"

"Yes, of course. By the by," Becca began carelessly as she steered the older woman through one of the French doors, "thank you for introducing us to Mr. Carouthers. Such a delightful man."

"Yes, he is, is he not? He is a distant connection, but I was glad to do what I could for him."

"I understand he's from the North Country?"

Lady Sandifer frowned at Becca. "Mercy, no! Where did you get such an idea? No, the boy's from

Cornwall. Never been to London before, but he's taken to it wonderfully."

"And he has an estate in Cornwall?"

Enlivened by the cooling breeze, Lady Sandifer became more expansive. "Lawks, no. The boy has a mere pittance. Hopes to make his fortune through marriage. Well, and I don't see why not. He is a handsome lad."

"Yes, he is," Becca murmured. Her goal achieved, she added, "I believe I must go in, Lady Sandifer. I find the air quite chilly."

She slipped back into the ballroom, to be greeted by the sight of Lady Emily and Mr. Carouthers sitting together while the orchestra played a waltz. With their heads bent near each other, they gave an appearance of intimacy that she hoped no one else noted.

She went to Lady Wixton's side to await Emily's return, resolved to keep close watch on the younger lady the rest of the evening. Catching sight of Lord Deveril, a friend of Lord Roth's whom she knew to be an honorable gentleman, she signalled a desire to converse with him.

He wandered to her side, bowing. "At your service, Mrs. Dunn. How are you this evening?"

"Very well, Lord Deveril. Have you seen Sir Anthony?"

"Well, yes, but not here. We had dinner together earlier."

Becca's eyes widened. "Do you mean he is not coming?"

The man looked uncomfortable. "Mrs. Dunn, he said he did not intend to show himself this evening. It seems he and Lady Emily, er—"

"Yes, I know," Becca interrupted, rescuing Lord Deveril from his embarrassment. "Oh, dear."

"I shall be glad to assist you if aught is amiss."

"Lady Emily allowed a Mr. Carouthers to sign her dance card twice, but I would prefer that she not dance with him again. I don't know how to bring it about, however."

"I do not know this Mr. Carouthers."

"He is sitting with her now across the room. He is—he is a fortune-hunter, my lord, though I know I should not say so."

Lord Deveril threw back his shoulders. "I warned Lucas they were everywhere. Never mind, Mrs. Dunn. I shall sweep her away before he can come to claim her."

"Thank you, my lord. I am sure Lord Roth will be most grateful."

"Where is he, by the way? I thought he usually shadowed the two of you about Town." Lord Deveril looked over his shoulder as if he expected to discover his friend nearby.

"He is escorting his mother to the theatre this evening and could not accompany us."

"Deuced odd, his attending all these parties. Most of the time you can't drag him out and about. The company must be of greater interest this year."

Becca's cheeks flamed as Lord Deveril accompanied his remarks with a wink. She was relieved when the music stopped.

"What dance did Carouthers sign up for?" Lord Deveril asked.

"It was number eight, I believe." Becca knew for certain because she had looked over Emily's shoulder.

"Don't you worry, my dear. I'll fix things all right and tight."

Lord Deveril was true to his word, and swept an unhappy Lady Emily onto the floor from under Mr. Carouthers's nose. Lord Deveril's rank and social standing made it impossible for the newly arrived Mr. Carouthers to raise much of a protest. For the rest of the evening he hovered about his quarry, but her dances were all promised.

On the way home, Becca held her tongue. Lady Emily's mood would not be receptive to any strictures on her behaviour or the fact that she had disobeyed her brother.

The next morning, Becca did not go down to breakfast. Instead, she took tea in her room and waited for word that Lady Roth was awake. When Eva came for her, she hurried to lay the trouble before Lady Emily's mother.

After telling Lady Roth exactly what Lady Sandifer had said, as well as revealing the man's lies from the previous day, Becca then asked for assistance.

"I do not know how to convince Emily to avoid him, Aunt Catherine. What shall I do?"

"I doubt anyone could convince my stubborn

daughter to do anything. Hmm." Setting the breakfast
tray aside and throwing back the covers, Lady Roth
held out a hand to Becca. "It is time for my regimen,
my dear. If you will help me, I shall try to find a way
out of this coil."

"Of course, my lady." Under the doctor's orders,
Lady Roth struggled to walk each morning. Though
it was painful at first, her limbs seemed to be gaining
strength.

As they slowly crossed room, Lady Roth gasped,
"I believe we must, ah, approach the difficulty from
Mr., uh, Carouthers's side." She paused to take a
deep breath. "*Aah.* Sometimes I think I'll never walk
properly again."

"Nonsense, Aunt. You have made remarkable progress."

Lady Roth grinned at her. "Yes, I have, have I not?
When I finish this torture each day, I think of that."
She moved slowly forward again.

"What did you mean about approaching our difficulty from Mr. Carouthers's side?" Becca asked, anxious to find a solution.

"If we cannot, ah, discover a way to prevent Emily
from seeking out Mr. Carouthers, we must prevent
him from seeking out Emily. Aah!"

Becca shored up Lady Roth's trembling body.
"But I don't see how—"

"That," she panted, "is because you are not as
crafty as I am, my dear." She sank down on the

chaise longue. "That will do for today. Fetch me another cup of tea."

Becca eagerly did so and then sat down on a nearby stool. "How?"

Lady Roth smiled at her brief question. "We shall simply offer him a more attractive catch."

"You mean find another heiress for him? Would it not be cruel, to betray another young innocent?"

"I would never do that, dear. I'm afraid I must ask you to participate in a small charade."

"Me?"

Lady Roth leaned back and closed her eyes. "I believe you will become an heiress in disguise—one immensely wealthy, helping us hide the fact that our fortune has diminished considerably. Shall you object to a pretence?"

Becca gasped. "N-not if it will aid us."

"I am certain you will make an excellent conspirator, my dear Becca. Our family connection will serve as a believable explanation for your generosity."

"Will Mr. Carouthers believe such a tale, and how will he learn of it?" Becca asked, worried about the details.

"Oh, of course he will believe it. He is a greedy man seeking an easy fortune. And I shall tell him our secret, of course." She smiled at Becca. "Child, I have always enjoyed theatrics. You will see."

"Yes, Aunt." Relieved to have a solution to a knotty problem, Becca only had one more question. "And will Lucas approve of our plan?"

"Good lord, child, I don't propose to tell *him!*"

"But, Aunt Catherine—"

"No, no, no! He will rant and rave, upset Emily and cause all manner of difficulty if we tell him anything. We shall handle the matter ourselves."

Lady Roth summoned Eva to help her dress, so that she might be in the parlour to receive any guests who might come calling. Both ladies suspected Mr. Carouthers would appear. Becca still wasn't sure how Lady Roth would set their scheme in motion, but she placed her faith in the lady's ingenuity.

When they reached the parlour, they discovered Lady Emily pacing the floor, dressed to go out. She started in surprise when the other two, her mother carried by Jem, entered the room.

"Oh! H-hello, Mama, Becca."

"Hello, dear. Are you going out?"

Becca remained silent, waiting for Emily's response.

"I—I thought I might go out for a drive."

"What a good idea. It is a lovely day. Have you summoned the carriage? I shall just ask Murdoch to have Eva bring down my things. I should love a breath of fresh air."

Lady Roth was indeed a good actress, Becca decided. Her innocent response to her daughter's clearly clandestine plans was perfect.

Emily was trying to discover a good reply when Murdoch opened the door.

"Lady Emily, Mr. Carouthers is at the door. He said he has come to take you for a ride in the Park."

The guilty red flush in Emily's cheeks told the story, but Lady Roth continued with her play-acting. "What a shame. Shall we tell him we already have plans, my dear? Or would you prefer to invite him in for a cup of tea and postpone our drive until later?"

Lady Emily fell right into her mother's trap. "I think we ought to ask him in for tea, Mama. After all, he was kind enough to offer the invitation."

"How true, darling. I have raised a thoughtful child, have I not, Becca?"

Afraid Lady Roth was becoming carried away, Becca only nodded, flashing a warning to the older lady with her eyes.

"Murdoch, ask Mr. Carouthers if he would care to join us for tea."

The butler obeyed his mistress and soon Mr. Carouthers, slightly confused by the effusive greeting he received, joined them. Before Lady Roth could make any progress with her plan, several other callers appeared, both more welcome in Becca's mind.

Sir Anthony and Lord Deveril joined the others around the tea table, and the conversation remained general. Though Becca felt as if she were on pins and needles, Lady Roth seemed perfectly content and chatted easily with all three gentlemen.

After a few minutes, however, she turned to Becca. "My dear, why don't you find Lucas and tell him his friends have come to call. I'm sure he will wish to visit with them.''

Becca didn't want to leave. She was sure Lady Roth was putting her plan into action, and she wanted to watch her. However, she could not disobey such a direct order. ''Yes, Aunt.''

As she left the room, she heard the older lady ask, ''Mr. Carouthers, could I trouble you to push my chair over to the sunlight? I feel a little chilled this morning.''

Becca rushed over to Murdoch. ''Is Lord Roth in the library?''

''Yes, Mrs. Dunn, but he—''

Becca did not wait for his words. She wanted to hurry back to the parlour. When she reached the library door, she knocked and then opened the door almost immediately. Much to her dismay, she discovered Lord Roth had company.

''Oh! I'm sorry, my lord, I—''

''Come in, Mrs. Dunn. I was just about to ring for Murdoch and ask him to summon you.''

Lord Roth's face was stern and unwelcoming. Mr. Arbuthnot, his visage almost green with nervousness, stood silently as both men awaited her entry.

Becca's glance darted from one man to the other. She didn't want to sit down. She longed to return to the parlour. But again, she had no choice.

''Yes, my lord?'' she asked quickly as the gentlemen sat down after her. ''Your mother would like you to come to the parlour to greet some callers.''

"I believe that can wait. Mr. Arbuthnot has something to discuss with you. Shall I leave you alone, sir?"

Becca stared at Lucas. Why would he suggest such a thing? Suddenly realization struck her. She was about to receive another proposal. Her gaze flew to Lord Roth, her green eyes pleading that he not abandon her.

The young man, more nervous than his companions, blurted out the reason for his call, ignoring Lord Roth's question. "Mrs. Dunn, I would like to marry you!"

In contrast to her reaction to her first proposal, Becca was touched by the gentleman's regard. Mr. Arbuthnot might not be very old or very wealthy, but he was a sincere young man in the throes of his first real passion. She smiled gently at him. "Sir, I am truly honoured, and I find you a kind gentleman, but I fear I am too old to be your partner for life. I must refuse."

It took several minutes for Becca to convince the young man that his suit was hopeless. Lord Roth watched her struggle to avoid injuring her suitor's feelings with appreciation. He had felt reasonably certain she would reject her first proposal. Tyndall was not a catch in most people's eyes. But Mr. Arbuthnot, while not wealthy, had a reasonable competence and was a gentleman.

The agony he'd suffered waiting for her reply told Lord Roth he was far too interested in his sister's chaperon. But he stared at her beautiful face, filled with compassion for the gentleman beside her, and knew he had no choice. Nevertheless, how he would discover a solution to the difficulty of proposing to her while she lived under his roof, he did not know.

An embarrassed Mr. Arbuthnot interrupted his thoughts by mumbling an apology and fleeing the library.

"Oh, dear," Becca murmured. "I tried not to—"

"You did everything you could, short of accepting his offer, my dear. Do not hold yourself responsible." He smiled at her and wished he had the freedom to offer his heart as the younger man had.

"No, but—but he is a sweet boy."

"He is your age, four and twenty."

He watched in amusement as the lady's cheeks flooded with colour. Surely she was not embarrassed that he knew her age? "My mother told me. I hope you do not mind."

"No! No, not at all. Oh! I must return to the parlour. Your mother wanted me to tell you Sir Anthony and Lord Deveril have come to call. She thought you might enjoy visiting with them."

"Of course I shall join you. I haven't seen Tony since he and Emily had their spat yesterday. Did they come to terms last evening?"

Becca looked at him in surprise. So much had occurred since then, she hadn't realized Lord Roth would not be privy to it. She stood and turned to the door before answering, "No, Sir Anthony did not attend the same entertainment as we did last evening."

He caught her arm as she would have opened the door. "Do you think their argument was serious?"

"I do not think so, Lucas. But I believe we should hurry to the parlour."

His eyes narrowed with curiosity as he looked at her, but he nodded in agreement and held the door open for her, much to Becca's relief.

Anxious to see what had happened during her absence, Becca sped down the hall, Lord Roth in close pursuit.

When they opened the door to the parlour, Lord Roth had almost come to expect that some disaster or other awaited him. However, he only saw five people having tea.

Lord Deveril and Sir Anthony were entertaining his sister. He was relieved to discover she and Tony were at least speaking to each other. When he turned to observe the room's two other occupants, he frowned as he realized his mother was enjoying a tête-à-tête with the man he'd intended to investigate.

"Good day," he called, attracting everyone's eye.

Various responses were given, but Lord Roth kept his gaze on his mother and her companion. Mr. Carouthers only nodded to him, but he excused himself from Lady Roth's side and hurried over to Becca as if she were the only person in the room.

"Mrs. Dunn, I missed your shining beauty. Thank God you have returned."

He drew her hand to his lips before she could pull it away. As he bowed over it, Becca's startled gaze met Lady Emily's.

CHAPTER ELEVEN

"I HAVE ONLY been absent a few moments, sir," Becca said, snatching her hand from beneath Mr. Carouthers's lips.

"Even a moment without your radiant presence is like time spent in a dark dungeon!" he exclaimed.

Consternation marked Lord Roth's face as he stared at the man. Before he could speak, however, Mr. Carouthers continued.

"May I escort you for a drive in the Park?"

Becca saw the shock on Lady Emily's face and wished they could have avoided hurting her. But their seeming betrayal was only to assist Emily, she reminded herself. "Thank you, Mr. Carouthers. That would be delightful."

"Mrs. Dunn, I do not think my mother can spare you for such an activity this afternoon." Lord Roth's voice was coloured with his displeasure.

Becca stood silently, unsure how to respond. If she didn't offer some kind of encouragement to Mr. Carouthers, he would turn back to Lady Emily. And it was the outside of enough that Lord Roth thought he had to manage her every waking moment as if she were all about in the attic. He seemed surprised when she glared at him.

Lady Roth rescued Becca from her difficulties. "Nonsense, Lucas. I can spare Becca for a ride in the Park. It will do her good." She beamed at her co-conspirator.

Anxious to escape Lord Roth's condemning look and Lady Emily's unhappiness, Becca excused herself to fetch her wrap and bonnet.

WHEN MR. CAROUTHERS departed also, Sir Anthony turned to Lady Emily. "My lady, I would enjoy taking you for a drive if Lord Deveril would not mind."

"'Course not," Lord Deveril said helpfully. "Be glad to walk to the club."

Embarrassed by the earlier events, her pride severely injured, Lady Emily intended to refuse the invitation. Her mother, however, forestalled a cowardly retreat.

"How delightful, Sir Anthony. Of course she will accept. Emily, dear, go fetch your things."

When Emily rose to obey her mother, Sir Anthony released his pent-up breath. He had feared her refusal.

Once Emily disappeared, he turned to his friend. "Lucas, I had intended to hold back offering for Lady Emily, but I can wait no longer. I am afraid someone will snatch her from me. Do I have your permission to pay my addresses to her?"

Everyone's delight was palpable. While Lord Roth was signifying his approval, Lord Deveril thumped his friend on the back and Lady Roth stretched out a hand to welcome Sir Anthony into the family.

"Here now, it is too soon for congratulations," he reminded them. "She might turn me down."

"We shall lock her in her room and give her only bread and water until she capitulates," Lady Roth pledged with a giggle. At Sir Anthony's horrified stare, she added, "I am only teasing, Sir Anthony. Emily shall choose her own husband. But I hope she is as wise as I think she is."

"My sister could not be so mutton-headed as to turn down such an offer," Lord Roth agreed. "Besides, Tony, I believe she truly cares for you."

His cheeks flushed, Sir Anthony allowed hope to rise at his friend's words. When Emily entered the room at that moment, he eagerly jumped to his feet.

"I am ready, Sir Anthony," she said. As he strode towards her, she raised her eyes to look at the other occupants of the room. Her gaze widened as all three beamed at her. Looking over his shoulder, Tony decided the sooner they departed for their ride, the better. Another moment, and those left behind would do the proposing for him.

Once they were settled in his curricle, Lady Emily asked, "Why were they all smiling so?"

"Dev just told an amusing tale."

"What was it?"

Desperately searching for a response, he was struck with inspiration. "I cannot really say. I was thinking only of you."

Their eyes met and Sir Anthony made no attempt to hide his longing. Lady Emily's cheeks flooded with colour and she looked down at her pale pink gloves.

Sir Anthony cleared his throat. "I hope you were not too disappointed that Mr. Carouthers—that is, I am certain Mrs. Dunn has no interest in the gentleman."

In a small voice, Lady Emily confessed, "No, I am sure she does not. And it does not matter. I only flirted with Mr. Carouthers because he flattered me and—and I was jealous."

Sir Anthony's fists jerked the reins so tightly his horses protested. "Jealous?"

"Sir Anthony?" A female voice drew their attention and he muttered several indistinguishable words under his breath.

"Good day, Mrs. Lamprey, Miss Lamprey."

The rather stout lady leaned over the side of her cabriolet, and Sir Anthony had an awful vision of the carriage tipping with the ill-distributed weight.

"Are you driving in the Park this afternoon? We are on our way there also. Would Lady Emily like to ride in our carriage? You could take Letitia up with you. She just loves curricles." The slender young lady cowered behind her mother, her face scarlet.

"Thank you, Mrs. Lamprey, but no, we are not going to the Park. Perhaps another day." Without consulting his companion, Sir Anthony slapped the reins smartly over his horses' backs and left the cabriolet behind.

"We—we are not going to the Park?"

"Not Hyde Park. Remain silent, if you please, until I manoeuvre past this wagon."

The unusual crispness of Sir Anthony's tone stunned Lady Emily, and she did as he asked. All the time, she wondered if her confession had given him a distaste for her. If so, she would retire from Society and remain a spinster all her days.

Such dramatic thoughts would have raised Sir Anthony's spirits. However, since he was not privy to them, he was left to concentrate on his driving while trying to control his rising hopes.

Soon he had left the crowded streets behind and was heading out of the city on the Tottenham Court Road. All he sought was a place where he could pop the question to the enchanting young lady beside him without interruption.

Finally he pulled the curricle to the side of the road and wrapped the reins around the brake.

"Why are we stopping here?" Lady Emily asked.

"Because I can wait no longer. Lady Emily—"

"Need some 'elp, guv'nor?"

Sir Anthony almost fell from his high perch. When he'd righted himself, he discovered a grizzled man in a much-travelled wagon watching him with puzzled eyes.

"No, thank you for your concern, but there is nothing the matter."

The man, instead of driving on, eyed Lady Emily

carefully. "L'dy, if there be a problem wi' this gent, ye've only to say the word. I'll—"

"No!" Lady Emily quickly responded. She did not want to hear what the man would willingly do to Sir Anthony. "Thank you so much, but I assure you I am fine."

Wiping his hand across his stubbled chin, the helpful man nodded and clucked to his horses. The two in the curricle sat in frozen silence as the wagon continued on its way.

Before Sir Anthony could take up where he had left off, Lady Emily interrupted him with a fit of the giggles. "Oh, dear, Sir Anthony, did you not tremble in your boots? I wonder what he might have done to you had I not pleaded your case?"

His shoulders stiffened as he said, "I can assure you I would have acquitted myself well, Lady Emily."

"Oh, I did not mean to offend you, Tony, I mean, Sir Anthony. Of course you would have—"

An eruption of noise stopped her words as the stagecoach came over the hill, its horses at a full gallop. Atop the box sat an elegantly dressed young man who had clearly imbibed too much ale at some point in his journey. Beside him rode the coachman, his eyes wide with fear as he clutched the side of the box.

The driver of the coach whooped drunkenly as he swept past the curricle. The noise of the coach, the driver's salute, and the cloud of dust raised by their passage, all spooked Sir Anthony's well-behaved bays and he fought to control them long after the coach had disappeared.

When he was finally able to turn his attention back to his companion, Sir Anthony discovered a disgusted young lady brushing the dust from her gown.

"My dear, I am so sorry. I only wanted a little privacy to speak to you. It seems we are always surrounded by others."

Lady Emily looked up at him hopefully, but she found him distracted by the approach of yet another vehicle. She heard a low groan escape his lips.

"Whoa!" the driver called to his pair as he spotted a curricle he knew well. "Tony, Lady Emily, what are you doing out here?"

"Lady Emily, you are acquainted with Mr. Whitechurch, are you not?" Tony mumbled.

"Yes, of course. Good day, Mr. Whitechurch."

"How d'ye do, my lady. Did your curricle break down? Or did one of your bays pull up lame, Tony?"

As he answered his friend's question, Tony leaned forward to unwrap the reins. "No, nothing is wrong. We are heading back to Town at once. Are you?"

"Yes, I am. Coming back from that cock-fight—ah, that is, from an appointment," Mr. Whitechurch said, casting an alarmed look at his friend's companion.

"Then we shall see you this evening, perhaps." Sir Anthony wasted no more time. He swung his pair around and turned back to London at a fast clip.

Lady Emily sat beside him, afraid to speak. Something had upset her companion, and she did not want to know what it might be. He could have decided to cast her off because of her flirtation with Mr. Carouthers. She had not intended it to go so far, but she resented her brother's high-handedness and had thought to show him her independence.

Sir Anthony did not halt his bays until they reached Roth House. He hopped down from the curricle and handed the reins to his waiting tiger. Waving aside the footman who appeared to assist Lady Emily, he swung her down from her high perch and led her up the steps without a word.

"Will—will you come in for a cup of tea?" Lady Emily asked timidly, watching his stern visage with hope.

"I am coming in," he replied without looking at her, ignoring the offer of tea.

When Murdoch opened the door, Sir Anthony marched her through it as though she were a recalcitrant schoolgirl. "Where is Roth?" he demanded of the butler.

"In the parlour, Sir Anthony."

Lady Emily noted that the butler was beaming at her, just as the others had earlier. She looked up at Sir Anthony, but he had no such happy look upon his face.

Murdoch swung open the parlour door and Sir Anthony pulled her along behind him, only to come to an abrupt halt as he saw the occupants of the parlour.

The same threesome was gathered around the tea table. However, in place of tea, they were lifting glasses of champagne into the air.

"Back so soon?" Lord Roth asked in surprise as his friend and his sister appeared. "I assume congratulations are in order." He smiled at them broadly.

Lady Emily stared at him, puzzled.

"Of course they are. The child has talked of no one else for weeks," Lady Roth assured her son as she brought her glass to her mouth and took a large sip. "I've never had champagne so early in the day," she added. "What a decadent delight."

"Congratulations, old man," Lord Deveril added. "Couldn't have chosen a more beautiful wife."

"*Confound* it! I haven't proposed yet!" Sir Anthony angrily protested. "Roth, may I entertain Lady Emily in the library, *alone?*"

"Yes, of course," Lord Roth answered, surprise on his face.

Without another word, Sir Anthony pulled Lady Emily after him down the hall to the peace and quiet of his host's library.

When the door closed behind them, he discovered he could not remember a word of his carefully planned speech. He dropped Lady Emily's hand as if it were a burning coal and turned his back to her.

"Sir Anthony?"

Her quiet voice brought him back to face her, his gaze reluctantly rising to meet hers. He felt sure she would be angry with him at botching his proposal so, even if she cared for him.

"My answer is yes."

The love shining in her eyes made his questions unnecessary. With a shout of joy that was heard down the hall, he swung his blond enchantress up into his arms. After several minutes of tasting her lips and holding her close, he discovered he did indeed still have questions.

"You are sure, my love? You truly care for me?"

"I should hope so, Tony! Otherwise, my behaviour has been disgraceful." The beautiful smile that curved her lips melted any doubts that might have remained.

"Why did you grow so angry that I danced with other young ladies?"

"I have already admitted to jealousy." Now that she was resting within the circle of his arms, Lady Emily no longer had such feelings.

"How could you think me seriously interested in anyone else when I hung on your every word?"

"You did not offer for me, however. I thought you did not care."

He tilted her chin up so he could gaze into her blue eyes. "You are very young, my love. I wanted you to care for *me*, not just accept an advantageous offer."

Her eyes wide with emotion, Lady Emily confessed, "I have loved you since you visited our estates last year to see Lucas. You paid me no mind at all, but I knew, even then."

He rewarded her honesty with a kiss before saying, "I watched you, my little love, but I could say nothing. You were still a child. But I waited for you to grow up." After another kiss, which grew more than a little heated, Sir Anthony suggested they return to the others in the parlour. "I believe we should join in their celebration before your mother indulges in too much champagne and leaves none for us."

"I think I would prefer to remain here," Lady Emily decided, her hands linked behind Sir Anthony's neck.

"As would I, my love," he assured her, kissing her lightly. "But your kisses are more intoxicating than the finest champagne, and we must save them for our wedding night. I can assure you that you will not go thirsty then."

"Then I shall have one last toast to our wedding now, my darling Tony," Lady Emily said, offering her lips to him one more time.

BECCA HAD NOT BEEN so bored since before she'd run away from her aunt and uncle. Mr. Carouthers had talked ceaselessly during their entire ride, offering her fulsome compliments that left her nauseated, or boasting of his many estates in the North Country.

She had spoken to every passing acquaintance, hoping to distract the man from his clumsy courtship, but nothing worked. She ignored his words as she calculated how soon she would be able to cast him out on his ear. Perhaps she could convince Sir Anthony to offer for Lady Emily soon.

When he reached for her hand, Becca almost fell from the carriage. She loathed having that man touch her. The thought of ever having to offer her lips to him was more than she could bear. But surely Lady Roth would not demand such a sacrifice from her.

And after suffering through this ride, she would return to Lord Roth's anger. He thought she had betrayed his sister by allowing Emily to fix an interest in Mr. Carouthers, and that she had then ignored his wishes by riding out with the man herself. Wishes! More like commands. He thrilled her with his every glance, but his orders were tiresome. Did he think she had no head on her shoulders? That she must be cosseted and guided through life? Her estates were as numerous as his, and her wealth perhaps even greater. When she gained control in six years, she would command as many servants as he.

"Do you agree?"

The insistent voice of the man beside her interrupted her thoughts. "I beg your pardon. I could not hear your words because of the noise of that last carriage."

"I asked if you agree that love can be born of an instant."

An instant? Yes, an instant. That first day, when Lord Roth had walked down the stairs, she had felt...

"Well? Do you not agree?"

Becca jerked her thoughts away from the man

awaiting her return. "Perhaps, Mr. Carouthers. But—but there must be other factors considered."

"I could not agree more."

The satisfied smile on his face made Becca wonder if she had agreed with other things while her thoughts were on Lord Roth. When Mr. Carouthers directed his carriage towards the gates of the Park, hope rose in Becca that her ordeal might be nearly at an end.

"Are we returning to Roth House?"

"Yes, Mrs. Dunn. I believe it is time."

His understatement almost brought a giggle to Becca's lips.

When they reached Roth House, Mr. Carouthers escorted her to the door. "May I accompany you inside? I would like to pay my respects to Lady Roth."

Such a reasonable request could not be refused, especially since it was important to keep him dangling until Lady Emily came to her senses. Murdoch guided them to the parlour, where they found the same five occupants as were there at their departure.

"Come in, come in," Lord Roth said, an expansive smile on his face.

Becca stared at him in fascination. Where had his anger gone? And his dislike of her escort?

"Yes, welcome, Becca. We are glad you are returned." Lady Roth motioned to Sir Anthony, and Becca was surprised to discover a bottle of champagne on the tea table. Sir Anthony filled two glasses with the bubbly drink and presented them to the new arrivals.

"Are we celebrating a special event?" Mr. Carouthers asked as he gladly accepted the offering.

"That we are, Mr. Carouthers. My sister and Sir Anthony have just pledged their troths." Before Becca could express her happiness, he added, lifting his glass, "A toast to Tony and Emily. Long may they prosper!"

Everyone raised their glasses, and Becca smiled happily at her charge, delighted that Lady Emily had chosen such a wonderful groom. Then it occurred to her that the engagement meant she need no longer encourage the boring man beside her. Her smile took on an added brightness.

"Well, this is good news," Mr. Carouthers said. "The air of joviality is refreshing, is it not, Mrs. Dunn? I cannot think of a more appropriate time for business of my own. Lord Roth, might I have a word with you in private?"

CHAPTER TWELVE

"You appear to be under a misapprehension, sir," Lord Roth said, staring at the man across from him in the library. "Mrs. Dunn is not an heiress, nor does she have many estates. She is my sister's chaperon and a distant connection to our family. Her dowry consists of five thousand pounds."

"I know that is what you have put about. Your mother told me. But it is not fair to keep her wealth a secret in the hope of claiming it for yourselves." As anger rose on his host's face, he swiftly added, "Not that I would not be above doing the same thing. After all, a fortune is a fortune."

Lord Roth shoved back his chair and strode over to the bell-pull. He remained silent until Murdoch appeared. "Tell Mrs. Dunn to come here at once."

He returned to his desk and stared into space, ignoring the man across from him. The sooner Mr. Carouthers was out of his house, the happier he would be.

The door opened and the woman occupying the two men's thoughts slipped into the room. "Yes, my lord?"

"Mrs. Dunn, Mr. Carouthers has—"

"Mightn't I make my offer in privacy, my lord?" Mr. Carouthers asked hastily.

"No."

Mr. Carouthers was surprised by Lord Roth's denial of a perfectly reasonable request.

"Mrs. Dunn is not going to accept your offer, so there is no need for you to see her alone."

"My lord!" two voices rang out in protest.

"Well, are you?" Lord Roth demanded of Becca, his stare a challenge.

"That is neither here nor there, my lord," Becca said determinedly. "This gentleman deserves gracious treatment, whatever my answer."

"I do not consider it in your best interest to be left alone with this man, and as your guardian—"

"You are not my guardian, and I am capable of handling my own affairs, my lord."

Mr. Carouthers, having observed the interchange with interest, felt he must intervene or he might be forgotten. "Indeed you are not...a child," he added as Becca stared at him blankly. "And I believe we would be most happy as husband and wife. Since your protector will not allow you to hear me out in private, I must offer my hand and my heart to you now." He sank down on one knee and extended his hand, a lovelorn expression on his face. "Will you accept my offer, Mrs. Dunn?"

She leaned forward to take his hand and Lord Roth's heart stopped beating; he was afraid she might accept out of pique. Mr. Carouthers took heart, but his hopes disappeared as he met her gaze. "No, sir, I will not marry you. But thank you for your offer."

"But my dear Mrs. Dunn, we would be so happy."

"No, sir. You mean to say you would be so happy living with what you hope are my riches. But I will not relinquish control of my fortune to any man."

"Mrs. Dunn, tell this idiotic man you do not have a fortune before he spreads such a lie throughout the ton," Lord Roth insisted.

"My fortune, large or small, is none of Mr. Carouthers's business, my lord. Nothing about me has aught to do with him."

Again feeling forgotten, Mr. Carouthers jumped up from the floor. "But you encouraged me!"

Becca swung round in her chair and fixed him with a chilling stare. "Sir, I danced one dance with you and rode in the Park for half an hour. If that is encouragement, there would be no wallflowers during the Season. They would all be pledged after the first week."

"You, sir, will leave at once," Lord Roth said, ready to rid Becca and himself of the man across from . . . . ave no reason to complain, since you . . . . ursuing my sister until this very morn. . . . . od and loomed over the man, and Mr. Carouthers paled.

"I do not believe such rudeness is necessary, my lord," Becca admonished. "I have rejected his offer. He will leave without your insistence."

"Why must you protest when I am only doing my duty as your guardian?"

"Because you are not my guardian!" she protested again.

"Perhaps not your legal guardian, but as a member of my family, residing under my roof, you are under my care."

"I am not a child and have no need of a guardian." Becca did not even know why she was arguing, but something about his manner set her off.

"I take my responsibilities seriously." He turned to Carouthers, who was still lingering, and nodded firmly. "Good day to you, sir."

The man did not wait to be asked again to leave. He stalked from the room, outrage on his face. When the door closed behind him, Lord Roth turned back to the young lady. "Why did you encourage him?"

"I did no such thing!"

He admired the raised chin, the anger in the green eyes. But he still wanted an answer to his question. "You intended to see him alone."

"Of course I did. I thought it only proper."

"You did not think it proper with Tyndall or that puppy Arbuthnot." She dropped her gaze and he asked again. "Why now?"

Lifting her chin, she faced him squarely. "Because I felt guilty. You see, your mother and I schemed against him."

"What do you mean?"

"When I discovered that he was indeed a fortune-hunter, I talked to your mother and she suggested we tell him *I* had a large fortune, rather than Emily. That is why he invited me to ride in the Park this morning instead of she.''

Lord Roth was beside himself with anger. He stalked across the room and back, his voice fierce as he demanded, ''You took your problems regarding my sister to a crippled woman who should be cosseted, not burdened with such things? Why did you not tell me?''

''Because you were too busy chaperoning your mother, fearful that she might be pursued by Mr. Ambrose!''

''It is my duty to protect my mother!''

''You are so protecting of us, so intent on treating us like ninnies, it is a wonder you have time to live a life of your own. We may be females, but we are not idiots, Lucas!'' Becca whirled to run from the room, driven by anger and hurt.

''Halt!'' Lord Roth boomed across the room. As she paused, he added in stern tones, ''You will bring all difficulties regarding my sister to me from now on. Is that understood, Becca?''

She stood with her head bowed, tears forming in her eyes. Finally, she turned to look at him. ''There will be no more difficulties, my lord, now that she is engaged to Sir Anthony. And I will not be responsible for her any longer, since my job is at an end.'' Without another word she left the library.

Lord Roth stood in his tracks, stunned. Her job was

at an end? She would leave? A protest rose up within him, but she was not there to hear his plea. And after their acrimonious words, she would not listen to him anyway.

His mother. She would know how to keep Becca with them until he could formulate a plan. He would ask his mother to help. Without a thought for his mother's need to be cosseted, not burdened, he rushed to the parlour.

BECCA SANK TO HER BED, tears streaming down her cheeks. Her position at Roth House was at an end. She had not considered that that would be the outcome of Emily's happiness until now. In a very short time, she would have to seek a new position. And continue to do so until she came into her fortune.

She would never see Lord Roth again. That thought filled her heart with woe. He had come to mean so much to her. The rustling of paper made her sit up suddenly. When she discovered that she was sitting on her new riding habit, delivered that very day, fresh tears mingled with traces of the old.

Now she would not ride with him in the Park on Satin, the mare he had provided for her. She had so looked forward to those rides.

A rap on her door followed by Emily's voice pulled Becca to her feet. She hastily wiped her wet cheeks with the back of her hand and opened the door to her friend.

"Lucas said you were leaving! Surely that cannot

be!'' Lady Emily stared at her before wrapping her
arms around the forlorn figure. ''Becca, you must not
leave. You are part of our family now.''

After hugging Emily, Becca backed away from her.
''No, not really. It is only a distant connection, even
though you and Aunt Catherine have made me feel
like part of the family. And now that you have become engaged to Sir Anthony, you have no need of
a chaperon.''

''But I am not to be married until the end of the
Season, and I shall need you at least until then. Please
say you will stay. I would like you to be present at
my wedding.'' Emily caught her hand and squeezed
it. ''You will promise to stay at least until then, won't
you?''

Becca steadied her trembling lips. ''Yes, Emily, I
will stay until your wedding. I promise.''

She'd received a reprieve from her banishment
from Roth House.

BECCA DID NOT SEE Lord Roth again until that evening, when the Roths dined *en famille* to celebrate
Emily's engagement. Sir Anthony sat beside his fiancée during the meal, and neither seemed aware of
what was being served.

Lady Roth and her son carried on a conversation
that demanded little from the engaged couple and
only occasionally a word from Becca. She was con-
scious of the man at the head of the table, but she did

not dare to look at him, afraid her feelings might show in her eyes.

When Lord Roth addressed her directly, however, she raised her green-eyed gaze to his.

"Did you receive your riding habit today, Becca?"

She could not keep the longing from her eyes as she answered. "Yes, I did."

"Would you care to put Satin through her paces in the morning, then? If we go early, the Park will be less crowded and we might even work in a gallop."

So she was to be granted her ride, a memory to treasure. "I would love to ride in the morning."

"Tony, would you and Emily care to join us?"

"Hmm? I beg your pardon, Lucas, I did not hear the question." Sir Anthony continued to look deeply into Lady Emily's eyes.

"Somehow I am not surprised. I said Becca and I are going to ride early in the morning. Will you and Emily join us?"

"Should you care to ride in the morning, my love?" Sir Anthony asked.

"If you would, Tony," Lady Emily responded, her gaze still fixed on him.

The other three could not keep amusement from their faces. The lovers scarcely knew anyone else existed.

"Very well, Lucas, we shall ride with you."

"I am not sure I should be pleased. As company, the two of you leave something to be desired. Becca, you and I must provide our own conversation on the morrow."

"I shall be so thrilled to be in the saddle again, Lucas, I will not quibble over a little conversation." Her cheeks glowed at the prospect.

"Neither will you hear any complaint from me, my dear," he assured her warmly.

"Nicely said, Lucas," Lady Roth commented. "I had begun to think you and Becca had argued, you were so stiff and formal with each other."

Lord Roth avoided Becca's eyes as he acknowledged his mother's deduction. "I will admit we had a small disagreement over your scheme concerning Mr. Carouthers."

"Why?" Lady Roth's smile conveyed her pride in their accomplishment. "It worked perfectly."

"It is my responsibility to protect my family, Mama. Becca should not have disturbed you with the problem."

"Nonsense. It is my limbs that are infirm, not my mind."

Before Lord Roth could protest further, as his expression proclaimed he would, Becca said, "Lord Roth does not consider a woman capable of protecting herself, Aunt Catherine."

"I did not say such a thing." He stared at the beauty who haunted his heart and mind. "I believe it is my role as head of the family to protect those who are in my care."

"Surely that does not mean we must avoid all thought?" Becca asked coolly.

By now, even the engaged couple watched the interchange with interest. Lady Roth's eyes were filled with speculation.

"Of course not. But you are not in a position to act, as men are."

"Only by reason of wealth," Becca replied, "and a society that says a woman is incapable of managing her own affairs. If I had a fortune and I married, I would be forced to hand control of it over to my husband. I would have no say in the decisions made to protect my estates. Is that fair?"

"You would not trust your husband to do what is best for you?" He watched her with a steady gaze.

"That is not the point, Lucas. Why must I relinquish control to another person when I am capable of determining my own future?"

"This is a ridiculous conversation. You have no fortune, and in any case most women are delighted to turn over control of their fortunes to their husbands."

Becca dropped her gaze but muttered, "It is easy to believe such a farradiddle since you yourself will never be called upon to do so."

Lady Roth laughed. "An indisputable point, Lucas."

BECCA ROSE the next morning and dressed with a mixture of excitement and trepidation. She and Lord

Roth had not parted on the best of terms the previous evening. But she wanted nothing to spoil her ride.

Attired in her green riding habit, her gloves and hat in hand, she descended for an early breakfast. Lord Roth and Lady Emily were already at table when she entered the breakfast parlour.

The smile that lit Lord Roth's face when she entered boded well for their ride. "Good morning, Becca. I applaud your choice of costume. Satin is fortunate to carry so lovely a rider."

She blushed at his compliment. "Thank you, Lucas. I am so looking forward to making her acquaintance."

"Is Satin Becca's mount?" Lady Emily asked unnecessarily, her interest on her breakfast.

"Yes. She is a beautiful mare, about the same size as Cricket," Lord Roth said, naming Emily's mount.

"Did Cricket travel well from High Oaks?"

"Yes, she arrived two days ago and is well rested. You had best make a good breakfast so you will have the energy to control her," he teased his sister.

An hour later, Lord Roth assisted first his sister to mount, and then Becca, his hands lingering on her waist as she made herself comfortable in the side-saddle.

"All right?" he asked, his gaze on her face.

"Oh, yes," she murmured, memories crowding in as she gathered the reins in her hands.

With a satisfied smile at the joy on her face, he mounted his powerful black stallion, Inferno and led the way to the Park, where they were to meet Sir Anthony.

Once he was able to place Lady Emily in Sir Anthony's capable care, he invited Becca to accompany him in a gallop. "We must do so before the gossip-mongers are out and about or you will be labelled as fast," he teased.

Becca didn't mind. She was too eager to put her mare through her paces. With a nod, she urged her mount forward and the two raced along the paths. Lord Roth held his stallion beside her mare, in spite of its desire to surge ahead. When he signalled the need to halt, Becca tightened the reins and Satin, obviously well trained, responded promptly.

"Oh, she's wonderful!" Becca exclaimed, her face filled with joy.

"Her rider is quite accomplished, also," Lord Roth said, his gaze on his companion.

"Thank you. I have been riding for many years."

"And must have missed it sorely." He reached over to place his hand on hers where it rested on the saddle. "We shall ride every morning if it is your wish."

Her blood surged through her at his touch and she shifted Satin slightly, forcing him to remove his hand. "I do not want to discommode you, Lucas. Surely a groom could accompany Emily and myself if you are too busy."

"I shall not be too busy. I enjoy a ride myself."

Though she feared his offer was another attempt to

protect her, she remained silent. She enjoyed his company too much to protest further.

They turned and retraced their route more sedately, seeking their companions, who had kept their mounts to a walk in order to enjoy each other's company. As they drew near Sir Anthony and Lady Emily, they realized the Park was growing crowded, as many riders joined the early-morning parade.

"Roth!"

Lord Roth acknowledged Mr. Whitechurch and several friends with a wink, and waited for them to reach him and Becca. He introduced the lovely widow to the riders and they all moved forward as a group.

"Need to ask you something," Whitechurch said, nudging Lord Roth away from the group. Lucas reluctantly drew Inferno to one side, allowing them some privacy for whatever question his friend had. He frowned, however, as he watched Mr. Barclay, a man he did not know well, immediately take his place beside Mrs. Dunn.

"So, YOU ARE the lovely widow everyone speaks about," Mr. Barclay said, leaning towards Becca.

Not feeling at ease in the man's company, she stared straight ahead. There was a look in his eyes that she did not care for.

"I am a widow, sir," she replied, keeping her eyes trained on Satin's ears.

He edged his horse closer to hers. "A lonely

widow, or does Lord Roth provide, ahem, companionship?''

Becca's response grew colder. "I am chaperon to Lady Emily, sir, and find her delightful.''

He leaned over to place his hand on her arm, and Becca jerked away, causing Satin to shy.

"That's a fine mount you have there, Mrs. Dunn,'' Mr. Barclay said, moving his horse near hers again. "Lord Roth has mounted you splendidly, it seems. Would that *I* could do the same,'' he murmured, a lewd grin on his face.

"Mr. Barclay, I would have a word with you,'' a steely voice interrupted as a black stallion forced its way between the two horses already occupying the path.

CHAPTER THIRTEEN

BECCA WATCHED in consternation as Lord Roth forced Mr. Barclay off the path before pulling his mount to a halt. She wanted to protest his high-handedness. Though she had not cared for Mr. Barclay's manner, neither had she needed to be rescued.

"Mrs. Dunn, Roth asked me to escort you to Tony and Lady Emily."

Looking up in surprise, Becca found Mr. Whitechurch riding beside her. In her distraction, she'd not been aware of his approach. "Very well," she replied coolly. Now was not the time to protest.

When Lord Roth joined their threesome a few minutes later, he found the riders ready to return to Roth House. He agreed readily, and they rode back through the now-crowded London streets.

As they entered the hall, both Becca and Lord Roth spoke.

"Lucas, I would—"

"Becca, may I—"

They both stopped in confusion until Lord Roth bowed and indicated Becca should proceed.

"I would like to speak with you privately," she said, avoiding his gaze.

He nodded before turning to Sir Anthony. "Murdoch will show you to the parlour. Becca and I shall join you shortly."

Once seated before his large desk, Lord Roth's face stern as he regarded her, Becca found it difficult to speak. She had to search for the anger she had felt when he'd interfered in her affairs again.

"Lucas, while Mr. Barclay overstepped the bounds of acceptable deportment—"

"That is a mild assessment of his behaviour, Becca," Lord Roth replied harshly.

Becca drew a deep breath before she continued. "I know it is unacceptable for a single gentleman to provide a mount for a lady, but he only expressed a wish to do so, he did not make an offer. I certainly would have made it clear that his words were offensive, had I had the opportunity."

"But surely you understood—" Lord Roth broke off and stared at her, and Becca wondered what had caused him such consternation.

"As I explained last evening, I am capable of handling my own affairs. I appreciate your…your concern, but your interference was hardly necessary."

His expression grew cold as he nodded. "Very well. I suppose you had to fend off suitors by yourself when you were tending the widow in Brighton."

Becca blinked before saying, "We did not go out much, but, yes, I managed my own affairs then."

"I believe I understand now, Becca. Shall we join the others?"

She told herself she was relieved to have Lord Roth agree not to interfere in her affairs, but somehow the sternness in his face froze her heart, and regret was uppermost in her mind as she entered the parlour.

WHEN LORD ROTH and Sir Anthony entered the reading room at their club several hours later, Lord Deveril and Mr. Whitechurch were waiting for them in their usual corner. Even before they were seated, Mr. Whitechurch was offering an apology.

"Lucas, I am sorry Barclay was part of our group. I had no idea he would overstep the mark so badly. I hope Mrs. Dunn was not too distraught."

Lord Roth shook his head, a frown on his face. "She was not, because she did not take Barclay's meaning."

"Not—" Mr. Whitechurch stopped and stared at his friend. "How could she not comprehend such an insult?"

"My question, also."

"What has occurred?" Sir Anthony asked. He knew Lucas had been distracted since their return from the Park, but his friend had said nothing.

"Barclay expressed a wish to…to mount Mrs. Dunn," Whitechurch muttered, embarrassed even to repeat the insult.

"The blackguard!" Lord Deveril exclaimed. "Did you challenge him, Lucas?"

Expelling a long sigh, Lord Roth said, "I wanted to meet him at dawn, but then all of London would know of it. I'm meeting him at Jackson's Salon shortly, where I intend to teach him how to deal with a lady.''

"And she did not comprehend the insult?" Lord Deveril asked wonderingly.

"Of course she would not," Tony said calmly. "She's an innocent. What does she know of mistresses and...and the physical act?"

The other two men were nodding in agreement, but Lord Roth shook his head. "She is no innocent, Tony. She's a widow, remember? That is, if her story is to be believed.''

Tony blinked in surprise. "I had forgotten. She seems as innocent as Emily.''

"Yes. And I am beginning to think her entire history was a fabrication to attain the position.''

The other three men leaned forward. "Surely she would not *lie?*" Lord Deveril asked.

"What makes you think her story is not true, Lucas?" Tony asked.

Lord Roth leaned back in his chair and rubbed his forehead. "Because it changes locale.''

At his friends' urging, he explained. "She supposedly kept house for a widow in Nottingham. However, I accidently named the town as Bath one day and she took no notice. Today, when I realized she had no idea what had occurred in the Park, I referred to her position with the widow in Brighton, and again she did not correct me.''

"That is not conclusive proof," Tony said

staunchly. "She has been a wonderful friend to Emily."

"I know. Perhaps that is why I did not seek out the truth at her first slip. I didn't want to know that she was lying." Lord Roth sat up, squaring his shoulders. "But now I have no choice. I must discover what kind of woman I have taken into my household."

"I will not believe ill of her until you have proof," Tony vowed, but his forehead was knotted in worry. "Besides, she is a member of your family."

"That is yet to be confirmed as well," said Lord Deveril grimly.

"How will you go about it?" Lord Deveril demanded. "Be happy to assist you. Rather like a treasure hunt, don't you think?"

Lucas stared at his friends, undecided. His thoughts were confused. He wanted to know the truth, but he hoped it would not reflect badly on Becca.

"Thank you for your offer, Dev, but I must proceed alone. In fact, I must first deal with Mr. Barclay before I can put any other plan into motion."

Since the other three had no intention of missing the exhibition Lord Roth would put on, they immediately rose to join him at Jackson's Salon.

BECCA DRESSED with great care that evening. They were attending the Westover ball, where Caroline Westover, a noted beauty, would be the centre of attention. Becca justified the choice of her most elaborate gown, a swirling cloud of silver tissue, in an effort not to be cast in the shade by the other lady's beauty. But in truth, she knew she hoped to restore some warmth to Lord Roth's eyes when he gazed upon her.

She had not seen him since they'd joined the others for tea in the parlour after their private interview. He had remained silent, his mien forbidding. She did not understand why her plea for independence should anger him so. Rejecting a would-be suitor was not that difficult.

When she joined the others in the parlour, her reward for the care she had taken with her toilette was a brief smile from Lord Roth before he calmly turned away. Her heart sank as she realized he had not yet forgiven her.

"Lucas," said Lady Roth, seated in her chair beside Mr. Ambrose, who was to accompany them that evening, "what is that mark on your cheek?"

Becca watched in surprise as Lord Roth's cheeks flooded with colour, causing the bruise his mother had noted to stand out even more.

"An accident at Jackson's this afternoon. It is unimportant."

"I do not understand why gentlemen must hit each other to enjoy sport," his mother muttered. "It is beyond comprehension."

"The art of defending oneself is ancient, my dear," Mr. Ambrose explained, a condescending smile on his face.

"Yes, but we could hope for at least a little progress in these enlightened times," Lady Roth returned with an even more superior look on her face.

"You should cry off any argument with my mother, Ambrose," Lord Roth warned. "I believe she and Becca are members of Mrs. Wollstonecraft's contingent."

Mr. Ambrose blinked in surprise and turned to stare at the demure lady beside him. "You would join that person? She thinks women are better than men!"

"No, Mr. Ambrose," Becca corrected, her chin high as she stared at Lord Roth. "She only believes women should be treated as people, not chattels."

Rather than respond to her words, Lord Roth smiled and said, "I believe we should depart now if we are to arrive before supper is served. I have heard Mrs. Westover is providing an excellent spread."

"By Jove, she always does. We do not want to be late," Mr. Ambrose agreed, rubbing his rounded stomach as if in contemplation of the feast to come.

Once they arrived at the ball, Lord Roth carried Lady Roth into the card room, where she and Mr. Ambrose intended to enjoy some fierce play. Sir Anthony marked his name on Lady Emily's card numerous times, which was permitted now they were engaged, and supervised those who would avail themselves of any other dances.

Lord Roth did not request a dance from Becca, and her heart sank as she concluded that he had washed his hands of her. She hid her anguish behind a quiet smile and scarcely noticed those who signed her card.

The second dance was a waltz, and Becca, after a rousing country dance with a youth who was no taller than she, looked at her card to see who her next partner might be. To her surprise and consternation, she discovered Mr. Carouthers's there. Yet she was sure he had not approached her that evening.

She quickly looked about, hoping to see Lord Roth, but he had his back turned to her and was across the crowded room. A voice at her shoulder told her it was too late for assistance in any case.

"Mrs. Dunn, I believe this is my waltz."

She hesitated. "I do not remember your signing my card, sir."

"You were quite distracted when you first arrived." Mr. Carouthers stood waiting, his hand extended.

With a deep breath, Becca placed her hand on his arm. After all, it was only one dance in a crowded ballroom. What could happen?

Mr. Carouthers swung her round the room, spinning her excessively, to Becca's way of thinking. As she passed one group, startled blue eyes met hers and Lord Roth frowned with irritation.

Becca closed her eyes, not wanting to face the furious question in his. Hoping the music would end soon, she followed her partner's lead and tried to forget his identity.

Just as she felt sure the music was finishing, Mr.

Carouthers swept her through French doors out onto a large balcony. "Sir! I protest! Unhand me at once."

"That I cannot do, my pretty one," he said quite pleasantly. At the same time, he forced a handkerchief into her mouth and deftly twisted her wrists behind her. Since her shrieks were muffled by the cloth and the music, her only recourse was to kick at her assailant as he tied her hands. It was no use; the villain managed to avoid her flailing limbs.

Turning her round once her hands were bound, he threw her over his shoulder and slipped over the balcony ledge to the grass several feet below. Becca's head struck the balustrade during their descent and she knew nothing else.

RAGE EXPLODED in Lord Roth when he saw Becca spinning about the dance floor in Mr. Carouthers's arms. How could she accept a dance from the man after all that had happened? Roth knew, however, that Becca had likely done it just to prove to him that she could make her own decisions.

At first, he had decided he would ignore her for the rest of the evening. But he could not bear to abandon her. If she was as innocent as he thought her, she might have need of him, whether she wanted his assistance or not.

The gentlemen with whom he had been conversing were surprised when he interrupted their dialogue. "Excuse me. I must speak to my sister." Without another word, he walked away.

Across the room, he discovered Tony and strode to his side. Then he turned to locate Becca on the dance floor. "Did you notice Becca's current dancing partner?"

"No. Someone interesting?"

"Mr. Carouthers."

"No! I am surprised. I thought—"

"I cannot see her!"

"She is probably on the other side of the room. It's dashed difficult to find anyone with all these people whirling about."

Lord Roth gave credence to Tony's words, but he stared intently at the dancers, seeking the silver gown and glorious crown of dusky curls. As the music drew to a close and the dancers strolled from the floor, he clutched his friend's arm. "Tony, she is not here!"

His eyes on Emily, who was approaching, Tony murmured, "Perhaps the clumsy oaf stepped on her gown. She is probably in one of the waiting-rooms having it mended."

Lucas reached Emily before Tony even realized he had moved. "Go and search the waiting-rooms for Becca. Let me know as soon as you have found her."

One look at her brother's face convinced Emily not to ask questions. She sped away to do his bidding. He turned back to Tony. "Please go to the card room and see if she is with my mother. I shall check the supper room."

"Haven't started serving yet," Tony protested, but when Lucas only turned and hurried away, he shrugged his shoulders. "Don't know what all the fuss is about," he muttered.

Lord Roth was waiting for both of his assistants when they returned, but neither had discovered Becca's whereabouts.

"Tony, look out on the balconies while I ask our coachman. Perhaps she took ill and went home."

Lady Emily accompanied her fiancé, not averse to a little romance in the moonlight. Though she knew her brother was alarmed, she did not quite believe anything could be wrong.

"Tony, why is Lucas so upset? Have he and Becca had another quarrel?"

"No. He saw her dancing with Mr. Carouthers."

"Mr. Carouthers? I would not think she..."

Tony pulled her through one of the French doors, and the beauty of the night distracted her. "Oh, Tony, isn't it lovely out here?"

"Yes, my love, but we really must find Becca."

"Yes, of course, I—" She stopped abruptly as she tripped over something. "What is this?" She lifted a silver reticule, one she had seen only a little earlier that evening. "Tony! It is Becca's!"

"You are sure?" he asked, even as he looked at the object. Swift deduction carried him to the balcony edge. In the distance, he saw a hackney cab just disappearing from view.

"Come. We must find Lucas."

In front of the town house they found Lord Roth in conversation with their coachman. "Lucas, we found her reticule! From the back garden I saw a hackney cab just driving out of sight.''

Lord Roth's face paled but he wasted no time. ''See that my mother and Emily arrive home safely.'' He turned and rushed into the street to hail a hackney himself. Their coach was too boxed in to be of any use.

''Tony, go with him!'' Emily begged. ''Mr. Ambrose will see Mama and myself home. You must help save Becca.''

With a nod, Tony squeezed her hand and ran after his friend. Emily watched him go and then turned to find her mother and inform her of the headache that would necessitate their leaving the party early.

CHAPTER FOURTEEN

SEARING PAIN greeted Becca's return to consciousness. She kept her eyes closed as memory flooded back, warning her of her precarious circumstances. The jolting movement of a carriage, along with its unsavory scent, told her she was probably in a hackney.

Opening one eyelid slightly, she spied the gentleman who had caused her difficulties. Mr. Carouthers was sitting in the other corner of the hackney looking quite pleased with himself.

As well he might, Becca thought forlornly. If he managed to marry her, he would be a wealthy man. And she would lose control of her inheritance and her independence. Well, she would refuse to marry him, no matter what he did to her, she resolved.

Determined to save herself, Becca carefully surveyed her choices. The man had not bound her ankles. She slumped down a little more, ready to attack, when a shout from above halted her.

"Guv'nor, there be another coach after us, shoutin' for us to stop."

Mr. Carouthers lost his self-satisfied air as he sprang forward to stick his head out the cab window.

Presented with such a perfect target, Becca could hold back no longer. With both feet, daintily clad in satin slippers, she kicked Mr. Carouthers with all her might. The latch gave way and he fell out, onto the ground below.

The coachman, turning back to look at his pursuers, noticed the exit of his paying passenger and hauled back on the reins. Becca, unprepared for their rapid halt, slid forward onto the floorboards.

Almost immediately, amid shouts and the jangling of harnesses, Lord Roth appeared at the open door of the carriage. "Becca! Are you all right?"

He scrambled onto the seat and pulled her upright. When she nodded but said nothing, he gently pulled the cloth from her mouth with a muttered curse. She coughed and swallowed several times before she could speak. In the meantime, he untied her hands and clasped her to him, his arms holding her close.

Becca had no objection to her latest situation. In fact, she found Lord Roth's chest a most admirable resting place for her racing heart. She eased her arms free of his and raised them to his shoulders, returning his embrace. Warm lips caressed her brow. When they reached her temple, however, she could not hold back a whimper. Lord Roth had found the bruise she'd sustained descending from the balcony.

"What is it, my love? Did he hurt you?"

"I—I hit my head. Lucas, how did you find me so quickly?"

He gathered her tightly against him once more. "I

saw you dancing with that man and I was concerned that you might not be able to handle him as easily as you thought. I lost sight of you temporarily and then, when I could not find you, Tony and Emily helped me search.''

Lord Roth took heart when she did not move away from him, but he could not resist teasing. ''Do you again object to my interference in your affairs?''

She was shaking head against his chest when Tony interrupted their solitude. ''Lucas, I've got Carouthers here. What shall I do with him?''

''I'll deal with him. Escort Mrs. Dunn home, please, Tony.''

As Roth released Becca to climb out of the hackney, she protested, clutching his coat. ''No! Lucas, I will not leave you here alone with that scoundrel.'' She realized her plea was having no affect on Lord Roth, so she turned to his companion. ''Tony, please, we must not desert him!''

''Becca's right, Lucas. We cannot leave you here alone.'' Lucas detached himself from Becca, and stepped out of the hackney. Tony swiftly drew his friend aside and said in an undertone, ''Besides, you have already beaten one man today for her.''

Lord Roth did not respond to his friend's teasing, and said only, ''He will not escape scot-free from such scandalous behaviour.'' His words were laced with deadly intent.

''Of course not,'' Tony agreed, ''but his sudden exit from the coach has already done him considerable damage. He may have even broken his arm. Allow him to go on his way, with the threat to reveal his heinous crime should he ever show his face in London again.''

Lord Roth looked over his shoulder at Becca's anxious face and then stared at the man cringing against the side of the other hackney. ''Very well,'' he agreed tersely, and strode over to confront Mr. Carouthers.

Becca watched the three men as they talked, or rather as Lord Roth talked. Her spirits rose when Mr. Carouthers was shoved into the hackney and it rolled away. The other two then returned to hers.

Unfortunately, now that the initial shock had worn off, Lord Roth resumed a formality that contradicted his earlier behaviour. Becca assured herself she would not have assented to another embrace in any case, but she wished it could have been so. All three sat stiffly and silently after Sir Anthony asked about her health. It was a long ride back to London.

Lord Roth decided that when they returned home, he would demand that Becca be honest about her background. He needed to know all about her, in order to protect her sufficiently. And he intended to protect her!

WHEN THE WEARY TRIO entered Roth House, Murdoch murmured, ''Lady Roth is awaiting your return in the parlour.''

When Lord Roth would have continued on to the parlour with the other two, Murdoch held him back and added in a low voice, "Lord Dunlevy arrived shortly after your departure, my lord, and insisted on awaiting your return. I put him in the library."

Lucas frowned. He knew no Lord Dunlevy. "Thank you, Murdoch. I will go to the library as soon as I reassure my mother. Please prepare a tea tray for those in the parlour."

"I have already done so, my lord."

When Lucas entered the parlour, he found Becca the centre of attention. At his appearance, however, all conversation stopped. Becca's gaze was upon him and he found it difficult to meet her eyes.

"Mama, as you can see, our efforts were successful."

"Yes, Lucas, you were superb, you and Tony both. Thank God you were able to bring her back."

"In actual fact, I am not sure Tony and I were necessary," Lord Roth said, a smile on his face. "Becca had already rescued herself when we arrived."

Both Lady Roth and Lady Emily demanded an explanation, but he referred them to Becca and excused himself. Becca stared at him over their heads as he withdrew from the parlour.

When he opened the library door, he discovered Lord Dunlevy to be a man of middle age, his hair grizzled, his figure burly. He had never seen him before in his life.

"Lord Dunlevy? I am Roth. How may I be of service?"

The man stepped forward to take his hand. Lucas noticed the sobriety of his dress, its simplicity unusual for a peer of the realm.

"I am here on a sensitive matter, my lord. May I speak in confidence?"

Frowning, Lord Roth nodded agreement, but he wondered exactly what he was about to be drawn into. "I am not familiar with your title, my lord. Do you have estates near London?"

"No, my lord. My estates are in the North Country. I inherited my title three years ago from my brother, God rest his soul."

"What is this sensitive matter?"

"I have come in search of my niece."

As if he had taken a blow to his lower body, Lord Roth forgot to breathe for a few seconds. Then he gasped, "Your niece?"

"Aye. I finally traced her to London. Never thought she would come this far."

Roth studied the man's features, looking for some similarity to those of the person he suspected was the missing niece.

"And what led you to my door?"

"The girl is a distant connection of yours through her mother. Thought she might seek shelter here." There was an anxious expression on his face that reassured Lord Roth.

"I see. And your niece's name?"

"Lady Rebecca Dunlevy."

A titled lady. He ought to have known it from the

proud tilt of her head, her independence. She was accustomed to giving orders, not taking them. A deeply buried concern suddenly dissolved as he realized he and Becca were social equals. Now his plans, his hopes, might be realized with less difficulty than he had anticipated. His heart soared.

"Be at peace, my lord. Mrs. Becca Dunn has been living under my roof for several weeks. I suspect she and your niece are one and the same."

The man sighed deeply before saying, "So she is safe."

"Yes, though...yes, she is safe." There was no point in explaining how close Becca had come to not being safe that very evening. He walked to the bell-pull and summoned Murdoch, requesting Becca's presence when the butler responded.

"Please be seated. Mrs. Dunn will join us presently."

"She did not marry, did she? That is why she left home, you know. I arranged a marriage with one of our friends, and she refused to obey me. My brother was too lax as a parent." The man rubbed his brow wearily. "She should have obeyed me," he repeated stubbornly.

"Then she has never married?" Lucas asked, a gladness filling him. He wanted no other man to touch her.

"Nay, she would have none of James, and him a decent man, too."

The library door swung open and Lord Roth looked

into the eager gaze of the beautiful woman who had driven him to distraction for so long.

"Lucas?" she greeted him, not noticing the other man.

Lord Dunlevy slowly rose to his feet and turned to face her.

"Uncle!" she gasped, confirming Lucas's suspicions. Her face paled and she wobbled slightly. Though he moved swiftly to her side, she had recovered by the time Lucas touched her arm.

"Sit down, Becca. You have received a shock."

She did so, her eyes never leaving the older man. However, her composure was swiftly returning. "When did you arrive, Uncle?"

"This very day. Soon's I figured out where you had gone, I came straight away. You should not have run away, child."

Becca's chin rose and she stared at him coldly. "You gave me no choice."

"Here now, no need to air our dirty linen in front of Lord Roth," Dunlevy admonished her.

That was exactly what Lord Roth wanted them to do. He wanted to know why she had felt the need to run away. "I am at your service if I can be of assistance to you, Becca."

"It's Lady Rebecca," Lord Dunlevy reminded him firmly.

"Pardon, Lady Rebecca."

His offer was ignored as she turned away from both men, as if to gather her courage, before saying, "I will never agree to the marriage, Uncle, and if you force me to return with you, I will only run away again.''

"This time I shall know better, missy, and you'll not get the opportunity.''

Lord Roth cleared his throat. "I realize I am not an immediate member of your family, but we are connected, and I have acted in the role of Lady Rebecca's guardian for the past several weeks. Could one of you explain the difficulty?''

Lord Dunlevy remained stubbornly silent. Lady Rebecca looked at Lord Roth for the first time since entering the library, tears in her eyes.

"I apologize for deceiving you, Lucas. I ran away because my uncle wanted me to marry a man his own age, one who is a member of the Nonconformists, as are my uncle and aunt.'' She cast a sad look towards her uncle. "I do not condemn your way of life, Uncle, but it is not for me.''

"So you were not lying to Mr. Carouthers when you professed to have great wealth?'' Lord Roth said gently, seeking to confirm a growing suspicion. While her uncle was conservatively dressed, his garments were of the finest quality.

Becca's head shot up and she stared at the man she had come to love. "No, I was not lying. But I was also not lying when I told you I would marry no one. I will not give away my inheritance, the only thing I have left of my father. I am responsible for the people who live on my lands.''

"Nonsense," her uncle contradicted her. "You are a female and must have a man to guide you, to direct your affairs."

Lord Roth began to understand Becca's fierce independence. Her courageous spirit must have felt smothered in her uncle's household.

Becca leapt to her feet to whisper fiercely, "I will not marry that man!" before turning her back once again.

Lord Roth suspected she was hiding tears, afraid they would make her appear weak. He stood and came around his desk to face her, taking her shaking hands in his. "Becca, will you trust me to do what is right? I understand your fears. I promise I will not return you to your uncle if you—"

"Here now! You have no right to make such a promise!" Lord Dunlevy jumped to his feet in protest. However, when his gaze met that of Lord Roth, he slowly sank back into his chair.

"Go to my mother. Tell her the truth about your past, and wait there for me to come."

She nodded, saying nothing, her cheeks glistening with her tears.

"Promise me you will not run away until I have spoken to you."

"I promise," she whispered, and was rewarded when he drew her hands to his lips for a brief caress.

"I am not letting her out of my sight, my lord. I am her guardian. She will return home with me this very night."

Still holding Becca's hands, Lord Roth stared down at the man he was coming to dislike. "My lord, Lady Rebecca has given her word. Surely you don't doubt that she will keep it?"

Under the force of Lord Roth's stare, Lord Dunlevy cleared his throat and finally said, "As long as she's promised."

"Go, Becca. I won't be long."

BECCA DISCOVERED that Lady Roth had ascended to her bedchamber for the night when she returned to the parlour and found it empty. She went up the stairs slowly, her heart heavy. She saw no solution to her difficulties and doubted Lord Roth would be able to persuade her uncle to change his plans for her.

She had been so happy here at Roth House. She had felt as if she'd had a family again, as she had when her father was alive. Even more, she had come to love Lord Roth. He was a kind, loving man, devoted to his sister and his mother, even if his care was excessive at times.

And when she looked into his eyes, her heart raced and she longed to throw herself into his arms. The few minutes he had held her close this evening had been heavenly.

With a weary sigh she knocked on the door of Lady Roth's chamber. She did not look forward to confessing her duplicity to the woman who had shown her so much kindness.

Eva opened the door only a crack. "Her ladyship has gone to bed."

"It is urgent that I speak with her, Eva. Lord Roth told me to do so." The only way to persuade Eva to allow her admittance was to invoke Lord Roth's name.

"Wait here," the large woman muttered, shutting the door.

Only a moment later, it swung open again and Eva allowed her to enter.

"Becca? Is something wrong? Come closer, child, and tell me why you are here."

Becca walked over to stand by the bed where Lady Roth lay against numerous pillows, her gentle smile welcoming. How awful to repay such kindness with lies.

"Aunt Catherine," she whispered, sinking to her knees on the carpet by the bed, "I have a confession to make."

CHAPTER FIFTEEN

AFTER THE DOOR CLOSED behind Becca, Lord Dunlevy rose to his feet again. "My lord, the child belongs with me. I am her legal guardian."

Lord Roth reluctantly drew his gaze from the door to face the man. He stared at him for several seconds before retracing his steps around his desk and sitting down. "Be seated, Lord Dunlevy, and hear me out. I recognize your rights as the guardian of Lady Rebecca. However, I have a suggestion to make that might satisfy you."

With a grunt, Lord Dunlevy settled back into his chair, his expression making it clear he doubted Lord Roth's statement.

"Lady Rebecca has resided under my roof for several weeks. In that time, we have considered her a part of our family. My sister is expecting her to attend her wedding at the end of the Season. My mother and I had hoped to persuade Becca to join us at one of our estates, High Oaks." He paused, watching the other man's face for some appreciation of his words, but he found nothing.

"I understand your concern for Becca's safety," he went on doggedly. "But now that you have discov-

ered she is safe, could you not leave her in my care
for a few more months?''

"Nay, my lord. I don't doubt that you have dealt
kindly with the child, but she needs to be in her own
home. There are too many sinful ways in London.
Bad influence on her. Her father did enough damage,
educating her, treating her as if she should have a say
in her life.'' The man shook in head in dismay. ''The
child expects to give orders to God-fearing men!''

In spite of the seriousness of the situation, Lucas
could not hold back a smile, which he hid with a
cough. Lord Dunlevy's life must not have been easy
since he became Becca's guardian. The two had un-
doubtedly been at loggerheads from the first moment.

"My lord," Lucas tried again, "you must recognize that Becca will never accept your beliefs.'' When
Lord Dunlevy would have protested, he raised a hand
as he added, ''Your teachings have come too late in
her life.''

"Aye," the man agreed with a heavy sigh. "But I
must try. It is my duty. Perhaps when she marries
James, he will be able to sway her.''

"Lord Dunlevy," Lucas said, rising and coming
around his desk, "during the past month, I have come
to respect and love Becca. I have not spoken to her
of my feelings because she was under my care. Now,
however, since she has a true guardian, I would like
to ask for her hand in marriage.''

Lord Dunlevy's face showed his indecision and
Lucas added, ''I do not follow your way of life, my

lord, but I am an honourable man, and I would care for Becca all of her life.''

"I'll not lie to you, my lord,'' Dunlevy replied at last. "Acting as guardian to one such as Rebecca has not been easy. But I do my duty. I cannot feel leaving her here in London would be right.''

Gently, Lucas said, "My lord, I do not think Becca will willingly return to your estates with you. Would it not be better to leave her here, safe in my care, than to have her run away again?''

"I'll keep her locked up until her wedding. Then she will not be my responsibility. James is a good man.'' The stubborn tilt of Dunlevy's chin warned Lucas his battle would not be easily won.

"Might I suggest, sir, that you rethink your plan? Lady Rebecca is a most determined young lady. If she refuses to marry your friend, I do not think you are ill-spirited enough to force her.''

"There must be ways to bend her spirit,'' Lord Dunlevy growled. "I will pray.''

The thought of Becca's courageous spirit bent and broken filled Lucas with such anguish he barely held back a groan. He sent a few prayers Heavenwards himself. "My lord, I do not think you will even reach your home with Becca, much less bring her to the altar. She is a most determined young lady.''

"Is it her wealth that makes you so interested?'' Lord Dunlevy demanded suddenly, watching him intently.

Though his spine stiffened in anger, Lucas kept his

voice even. "I have fortune enough for any man, my lord, and will willingly provide you with evidence of it." He drew a deep breath. "I seek Becca's hand in marriage for one reason only. I love her deeply and forever. I can see no other woman at my side, now that I have found her."

"She won't be an easy wife. You would do better to find a more submissive woman."

"No, Lord Dunlevy. That is the beauty of my solution. You see, the very thing that dismays you about Becca brings delight to me. Matching wits and wills with her is a joy."

Lord Dunlevy stared at him, then finally shook his head. "Perhaps you are right, my lord. I don't want Rebecca to be unhappy. She is my niece, after all. Do you promise to lead a moral life?"

Lucas smiled, sensing victory. "I already do, my lord, but I shall understand if you wish to verify my character before you grant permission for the marriage."

"Nay, I can tell you are a man of your word. Very well, I'll give permission for the marriage."

Lucas stepped forward and shook the man's hand. "Thank you, my lord. I promise I shall care for her well."

"See that you do. We shall need to sign papers. I'll call on you first thing in the morning to—"

"You already have a place to stay?"

"Nay. I'll find a room somewhere."

"You will stay here with us, my lord. After all, we

are to be relations. In the morning, I shall summon my man of business, and whomever you choose to represent you, and make the final arrangements. If Becca agrees, of course. Do you wish to inform her of your decision to accept my offer?''

For the first time, Lucas saw a twinkle of amusement in the other man's eyes. ''Nay, my lord. I think I'll leave it to you to tell her. If she has any complaints, I'll hear about them soon enough. And I thank you for your hospitality.'' With a final shake of his hand, Lord Dunlevy turned to the door just as Murdoch appeared.

After giving instructions to his butler and watching the two men's departure, Lucas sank back down in his chair. He was relieved that he had convinced Becca's uncle to allow her to wed him. At least he had saved her from a life she detested. Now he had to ask her formally for her hand in marriage. Her words, declaring that she would never marry, rang in his ears as he considered her response.

Would she think, as Lord Dunlevy had done, that he only offered for her because of her rank and fortune? Since he had only just learned of her true identity, it would be a reasonable assumption. But, oh, how he longed to hold her in his arms again, to call her his own.

He slowly rose to his feet and followed in Lord Dunlevy's wake. Somehow he had to persuade Becca to accept him for her husband. Unfortunately, she might prove to be even more difficult to convince than her uncle.

"OH, AUNT CATHERINE, you are so kind to forgive me," Becca sobbed, her head on the bed as she knelt beside it.

Lady Roth's fingers caressed her silky hair. "Child, I admire your courage. In a like situation, I do not know that I would have had the strength."

Becca bit her bottom lip, anxiety welling up within her. "But it was all for naught. He has found me and will force me to return with him."

"Do not give up hope. Perhaps Lucas will find a way to forestall him."

Though she said nothing, Becca did not hold out much hope. A knock at the door brought both of them to attention.

"It must be Lucas. Let him in, child," Lady Roth said, crossing her fingers under the covers as Becca did her bidding.

Both women stared at him, waiting for him to tell them Becca's future.

"Your uncle has agreed to allow you to remain here, Becca," he said calmly.

Lady Roth clapped her hands together with a cry of joy. "Oh, Lucas, I *knew* you would rescue Becca again."

Becca did not express any enthusiasm or gratitude. She only waited for him to continue. After all, she knew her uncle well.

"He did so because—because he accepted my offer for your hand in matrimony." He watched as Becca's face turned deathly white. Fearing she would fall, he reached for her, but she jerked back from his touch.

His own face blanched at her reaction. Stiffly, he said, "If you would prefer returning with your uncle, of course, that is your choice."

The silence was fraught with tension as the other two waited for Becca's response. When she finally lifted her gaze to Lord Roth's face, there was no emotion visible. "No, Lucas. I accept your offer of matrimony." Without another word, she fled from the room.

Lucas and his mother exchanged startled looks, both thinking the same thing: this was a most unsatisfactory end to their evening.

FROM THAT NIGHT, Becca avoided Lord Roth at every turn. While her status had changed from chaperon to fiancée, from widow of a gentleman to daughter of a peer, from employee to future countess, she was not content.

A battle was being waged between her head and her heart. She loved Lord Roth. Had he loved her in return, she might have relinquished control of her inheritance with only a few qualms. But he had never expressed any warm feelings towards her. Only on the night he had rescued her from Mr. Carouthers had he shown any emotion for her at all.

And never, never for a moment, had he hinted that

he longed for any future with her until her fortune, her lands, her title, had been revealed to him. She realized he did not need her wealth. But men were acquisitive creatures. He did not find her unappealing, she knew, and when presented with her person *and* a huge fortune, he was willing to offer matrimony.

Many times she assured herself she should be grateful she was not to marry James Wilkes. His clammy hands and eager lips had repulsed her from the very beginning. Lord Roth, on the other hand, drew her to him like a moth to a flame.

Confusion reigned in her head as she faced her future. She was to give up control of her fortune, her lands and tenants, her life, to a man she loved who did not love her. She always ended her weary arguments with herself with a sob of despair.

In the two weeks following her uncle's departure, she grew more and more pale, and her clothes began to hang on her already slight frame. Her unhappiness was visible to those around her, but she would talk to no one.

Lucas watched from afar as his fiancée seemed to be slipping away from him. He had hoped to make her happy. Instead, he had only made her miserable. It pained him to see her so distraught. Feeling like a beast for forcing the marriage on her when she clearly did not want it, he finally summoned her to the library. Even though he loved her, he would not force her to marry him.

When she came into the room, a pale shadow of

her former self, he turned away from the window. "I hope I did not interrupt anything important with my summons, Lady Rebecca," he said formally.

"No, my lord."

He longed to hear her call him Lucas, as she had before his proposal, but she was always formal with him now. "I asked you to come because I—I wanted to offer you your freedom."

Her head shot up and she stared at him, but he could not read the expression in her eyes.

"I offered for you because I felt you would prefer marriage to me to your uncle's plans for you."

Becca's heart sank to her toes. He had admitted what she had already surmised. He'd thought to rescue her once more, even though he cared nothing for her.

He turned away, unable to meet her gaze. "I was clearly mistaken. In the past few weeks, you have demonstrated your unhappiness with our betrothal, and I am releasing you from it."

Becca's mind was awhirl. What would she do? Where would she go? Could she escape her uncle's reach? Could she live with the prospect of never seeing Lucas again?

The last question was the hardest, and she did not know the answer. But she knew it would be even more difficult to marry him, loving him as she did and knowing that he had no feelings for her in return.

Lord Roth watched her from the corner of his eye, hoping against hope that she would refuse to accept her freedom, that she would promise to marry him, to be happy.

Becca said quietly, "Very well, my lord."

He stared at her, the pain in his heart reflected in his eyes, but she did not look at him. Turning to leave, she stopped only when he asked, "What will you do?"

"Return to my uncle, my lord." Another lie, but she could not tell him the truth.

"I received the marriage-settlement papers from your uncle this morning. I'll send them back to him with a letter explaining our decision to break off the betrothal."

"No!" Becca could not allow Lord Roth to communicate with her uncle. "No, I shall tell him. In fact, if you do not object, I shall take the papers with me." Perhaps her uncle would never even realize the marriage had not taken place. At least she could delay his discovery that she had escaped him again.

Lord Roth frowned, not understanding her reasoning, but then shrugged his shoulders. "Very well. They are of no use now."

Becca picked up the stack of papers he indicated and fled from the room before the tears gathering in her eyes got the better of her.

She had protested Lord Roth's protection of her many times. Now she would face the world without it. She knew she would desperately miss his care, his presence. But better to face the world alone than with a husband who had married her only to save her from an unwelcome fate.

Trudging up the stairs, she entered her bedchamber and looked about her in desolation. She must pack, make plans for her departure. What little money she had would not last long. With a sob, she sank down onto the bed, dropping the papers on the floor.

After a few moments spent in tearful abandon, she gathered her composure. Crying would accomplish nothing. She must think logically. Her eyes lit upon the papers scattered at her feet. There might be a provision in the marriage settlement granting her spending money.

She gathered up the scattered sheets and took them to the window, determined to study the clauses that provided for the marriage she desired above all things but could not accept.

The legal wording was not easy to read, and Becca tired of it before long. But she persisted, anxious to find a way to forestall her uncle from reclaiming control of her life. Suddenly, she gripped the page she was reading and gasped. Carefully she read the words a second time, and then a third. With a shriek, she tossed the papers into the air and raced from her room.

LUCAS STOOD with his head down, ostensibly looking out his window, but in fact seeing nothing. He had lost her. She had taken her freedom and gone from his life. He could not imagine his future without her—

her smile, her teasing looks, her fierce independence. He had envisioned a life for them together at High Oaks, raising their children, sharing their joys and sorrows.

Now he was alone.

The door to the library swung open and then slammed behind whoever had entered. Murdoch must have let it slip from his hand. "Yes?" he asked in a weary voice.

"Why did you propose to me?"

He spun around, almost losing his balance, and saw Becca as he remembered her, her face vibrant, her shoulders back, her chin lifted as if facing a new challenge.

"Becca?"

"Answer me, Lucas. Why did you propose to me? Was it to rescue me one more time? Or to increase your holdings, to make you richer than you already are?"

He stared at her, his mind slowly awakening to the fact that she had not yet left, that he had been given another chance. Taking a step towards her, he said, "No. Though I would have done anything to keep you from your uncle."

"Then why, Lucas?" She took a step in his direction, her gaze never faltering.

"Because I love you, of course."

"You never told me that."

He took two steps closer. "No."

"Why?"

"When I told you your uncle had accepted my offer to marry you, you went deathly pale. You did not want me to touch you. I feared that you had accepted me because I was the lesser of two evils. I hoped...I hoped I could teach you to love me after our marriage."

He watched her draw a deep breath, watched the rosy colour flooding her cheeks.

"My lord," she began, and his heart sank at her continued formality. "You have complained of my independence. I promise to mend my ways after today, but first, I want to offer you my hand in marriage."

His heart leapt at her words and he closed the distance between them immediately, sweeping her up into his arms. After his lips answered her question with a kiss he wished would go on forever, he said, "I accept your offer, Lady Rebecca."

She rewarded him with another kiss.

When, many heated moments later, they were seated together on the leather sofa, he asked, "Why did you change your mind?"

"I read the marriage settlement papers." When he said nothing, she looked up at him, her eyes filled with love and tears of gratitude. "You gave me complete control over my dowry. You took nothing for yourself."

"You are wrong, you know," he said softly, his hand cupping her stubborn chin. "I took the best prize for myself."

"No, you left everything to my control. I read every word of it, Lucas."

He kissed her lips several times before he explained his meaning. "You, my love—my stubborn, independent miss—are worth more than any riches, any lands, any control. You are my prize, my joy, my life. You may remain as independent as you like, as long as you stay by my side, sharing my life."

Her arms tightened about his neck and she smiled dreamily up at him. "But I don't need my independence anymore, Lucas. I have your love."

"Always," he murmured, then confirmed his promise in a most persuasive manner. When he lifted his head once again, reluctantly, he said, "Now, let us go and inform my mother that she must complete the arrangements for our wedding at once. I refuse to wait any longer."

Becca, happy in his arms, didn't move. "Are you not concerned that the preparations for two weddings might be too much for your mother?"

He pulled her tightly to him, heartbeat against heartbeat. "No, my love. I have discovered the female of the species to be capable of ruling the Universe, not merely my household." With a sweet kiss, he added, "I can only say there could be no happier fate than to have you rule my household."

"I have no desire to rule over you, my lord," Becca said, her seductive whisper negating the formality of her address. "I only want to share your life, your love, forever."

"And so you shall, my heart. Forever and ever."